'Hodkinson has a light touch and a modest, self-effacing style.
He is a fine writer.'
– *The Daily Telegraph*

'Writing that is free of cliché and acutely on the money.'
– *Q*

'His prose is never less than first-rate.'
– *The Independent on Sunday*

'Everything written by Hodkinson is done with economy and
elegance, self-deprecating but never self-pitying'
– *The Times*.

'Hodkinson can weave poetry out of the mundane.'
– *Daily Mail*

'If, like me, you have a habit of lending your new favourite book
on the pretext of getting it back, you may think twice about letting
Hodkinson's beauty out of your sight.'
– *The Quietus*

'A deft writer, poignant and funny at different times.'
–*The Guardian*

'He has an evocative turn of phrase with an impressive economy of
language and the writing flows effortlessly.'
– *The Observer*

'Hodkinson writes quite beautifully, which means that those of us
with lesser gifts are given a glimpse into his soul.
It is a richly rewarding place to be.'
–*The Times*

'Pomona's impressive list of authors includes Simon Armitage,
Barry Hines and Trevor Hoyle. Hodkinson proves himself
worthy of such illustrious company.'
– *The Observe*

D1419075

THAT SUMMER FEELING

Mark Hodkinson was born in Manchester and has two sons. He has written for *The Times* for more than twenty years and has produced and presented documentaries for BBC Radio 4. His debut novel, *The Last Mad Surge of Youth,* was *Q*'s novel of the year and his sports memoir, *Believe in the Sign*, was long-listed for William Hill sports book of the year. He commissioned and edited the acclaimed biography, *JD Salinger: A Life* published in the United States by Random House. He has released records as both Black September and Black Sedan.

MARK HODKINSON

That Summer Feeling

POMONA

A Pomona Book
POM:28

Published by Pomona Books 2018
Suite 4
Bridge House
13 Devonshire Street
Keighley
West Yorkshire
BD21 2BH

www.pomonauk.com

A CIP catalogue record for this book
is available from the British Library

ISBN: 978-1-904590-32-3

Set in Linotype Granjon by Geoff Read
Cover design by Geoff Read
www.geoffread.com

Painting of the Caves of Drach by Terry Eves

Mad in England!

Printed and bound by TJ International, Padstow, Cornwall

Friday

Everything is appropriated. Taken, gone, owned. Before we'd been born or had properly woken up and learned that we could wheedle bits for ourselves, someone more powerful or privileged or presumptuous had already grabbed the best stuff, done it. They have it all now. It says so on paper or scanned into computer files: land, mansions, businesses, office blocks, industrial estates, everything — all theirs. The contracts and deeds are kept inside huge buildings where they have men in uniform standing at the front or sitting behind a desk or *work station* pretending they're there to help you, Sir or Madam, but actually keeping guard, sort of. We don't push past yelling that everything, the lot of it, rightly belongs to us—all of us, the people—because we're mostly shy and diffident and, of course, afraid of causing a scene. That's it, more than anything else; we're scared of causing a scene.

Loachy isn't. But he's a one-off. He's as sure of himself and as angry as he ever was: flying the flag and fighting the foe, still hating all those things you're supposed to hate in boiling blood for the rest of your life forever and ever, amen — inequality, racism, misogyny, bureaucracy, globalisation, the monarchy, the wealthy, interfering neighbours. He's as good as bald now. He shaves what hair he has left and often has little bloody nicks on his scalp, red and sore. It's as if he does it to jolt himself to life. Jab, jab, salve with vinegar. That's better, that's worse, hurting for the cause. Lately he's taken to wearing too-tight tracksuit tops, zipped up high, his face often bitter and stony as if he's walking defiantly into an icy headwind.

1

I first met him when we were doing A Levels at sixth-form college. He had long curly hair then and was often bedecked in rainbow coloured woven ponchos as though he'd been dressed by kindly stallholders at a craft fair. He was already joyfully vindictive to anyone he considered bland or conventional but the flowing robes softened the effect. These days he looks bloody mean. Imagine a drug dealer or a high up copper.

Last time he called round he banked his car on to the pavement. I went to say, 'Don't do that, the neighbours don't like it.' Too late, he'd abandoned the car and was marching up our drive. Within seconds I could see old Jack at his window across the way, doing his tut-tut face. That strip of land, adjacent to the pavement and (more or less) in front of his house: no vehicle except his shall park there, rules is rules. If one did, Jack, and possibly several other like-minded, community spirited neighbours, reserved the right to walk round and round the vehicle, staring hard into the windows as if it were an alien craft. And, lo, should it remain in situ until late, just past teatime say, parked like that, half on and half off the pavement, a danger to children and an inconvenience to pedestrians, they reserved the right to tip used tea bags on to the bonnet. Splat. That's what they do around here, straight from the pot. As if Loachy cared.

"Tough," he said.

Didn't even look behind him. 'Tough', simple as that.

You've got to admire him not giving a damn. I'm not sure it's good for his health, though. He's got skin the colour of corned beef and he's not yet thirty. And some of his artwork is peculiar and hostile. I remember once reading a pamphlet promoting an exhibition and it referred to his work as 'fevered'.

He was making a quick visit, dropping off a book he'd borrowed. I had the run of the house because my folks had gone away for the weekend, staying with friends at their caravan. This time Loachy had parked quite neatly. I saw Jack at his window. He nodded to me proprietarily as if to say, 'The lad's improving'. Loachy threw me my copy of Cesare Pavese's *The Beach*.

"Loved it," he said. "Thanks for the loan. I know the setting is very pre-war Italy but the way the characters think, the way they talk, it could be now."

He dropped into an armchair, big sigh. I was planning—possibly, maybe—to tell him about my girl trouble. They were his specialist subject, after all. Right back to the beginning, those first few days at sixth-form college, I'd seen him in action. The revolutionary zeal was set to a different beat, charm and flattery instead of confrontation. The girls in the refectory or at the bus stop knew it was front but he had a smile that said he knew it was and he knew they did too, no harm done. That smile could get him out of a lot of bother.

During his time at college he'd worked occasional weekends as a greeter in a car showroom. He'd take out his earrings, hang up the ponchos and slip on a grandad suit from Oxfam. Women seldom ventured in alone, so he assumed the two or three that did on an average Saturday afternoon were almost certainly single and fair game. He was nineteen then but easily passed for mid-twenties with his receding hairline and stocky physique. He wasn't conventionally good-looking. Everything on his face was large—eyes, mouth, nose, lips—so he was, I suppose, a caricature of masculinity. Once he'd discerned that the women callers weren't time-wasters or 'tyre kickers' (as they were known among the staff), he was supposed to direct them to a member of the sales team. His colleagues soon realised that this part-timer's patter was at least as good as theirs and left him to it. He'd wink as he showed an attractive woman around the latest models. They became used to him waving his phone at them seconds after she'd left, indicating that he'd got her number. They surmised that if he'd got the girl he'd also got the sale.

When he spoke about women Loachy talked it round that it was a perfectly reasonable adjunct to his self-proclaimed 'socio political stance', a sharing out of love and communality and a retort to the conformity of marriage and settling down. He was teaching odd days at the local art college so had a pretty flexible lifestyle. I asked him the current tally.

"Three."

Tuesday afternoon, he told me, was 'Jess time'. She worked at a travel agent's and was nearly forty. Her husband had floated off. I asked what this meant.

"He smokes so much dope that he's permanently out of it."

Laura and Becky were the others, both divorced with kids. They wanted a relationship, he said, but nothing too serious because they were reluctant to present their children with a new 'dad'.

"I respect that and think more of them for it," said Loachy.

"It shows they put their kids first, which is a good thing. Women keen for you to move in with them straight away and play dad to their kids are always a bit needy. Very needy, in fact."

I wanted to tell him about my situation but kept changing my mind. I was afraid to make it all more real. And it's not like on those television programmes or films where you're healed for sharing something, all set to move on. You're usually worse because you've made it a much bigger deal, a fire that was contained becoming out of control. Do you want to hear yourself so indecisive, trying to explain to someone how you got into a mess. Anything you do in life, you've got to at least try to sort out yourself. Also, I sensed he had a defined image of me as this steadfast, dependable one-woman bloke. That's how friendships work. When you like someone you become more of what they expect you to be, even if it's bending your personality or causing you to limit or select what you share with them.

I began talking to Loachy in a way that was surreptitiously designed to illuminate my own dilemma while focusing on *his*.

"Don't you feel a bit mean on the three of them?" I asked.

"They each know that me and them is not exclusive. I'm not deceiving anyone."

"Do they actually know about one another?"

"It's 2004, man!" he said. (We'd originally taken on the exclamatory use of the word 'man' as a parody of 1960s-speak but it had stuck, especially with Loachy.)

He continued: "People are sophisticated. They've developed understandings. They get by, clever people anyway, by deliberately

5

not asking, not filling in all the gaps. Women are good at that, knowing how to be in the moment, going off what they sense or feel rather than needing information all the time."

"Is it the sex mainly?"

"No. I like the closeness. That can be sex but the talking is fantastic, too. You know: really talking. I fancy them and they fancy me and that's enough to charge you up, remind you that you're alive. You don't have to be having non-stop sex. Blokes focus on that too much. They make out that their mistresses or whatever they want to call them are red-hot for it because they project their self-loathing and guilt on to them. It's cowardly. Most people want to feel wanted and cared for, listened to, and situations develop, often through no one's fault, where this no longer happens in their main relationship so they seek it elsewhere."

"Don't you feel sorry for their partners?"

"Becky and Laura are single. With Jess I don't feel guilt, if that's what you mean. If things were okay in her long-term relationship we wouldn't be seeing one another, would we? I didn't cause them to end up like this; I'm a symptom not the cause. The apple will only fall from the tree when it's ripe."

"So speaketh the wise man."

"I *am* the wise man. I've learned such a lot from being close to women, what they're about, how they think. One day I'll fall properly in love with someone but I'll take that as the end of one particular journey, where I've learned loads and had so much insight, and the start of another."

He put his head in his hands.

"Sorry about that," he said.

"What?"

"Going on about a journey. Everyone's on a fucking journey these days."

After he'd gone I texted Sarah and arranged to see her the next day. This settled me, having something to look forward to. I'm always like this. I need focus, as if I'm afraid of the wide openness of tomorrow, next week, the future. I sometimes actually gasp at this thought, as you might contemplating the vastness of the sea or sky or standing back from a tall building, feeling it could topple on to you.

I circled the kitchen table a few times where my papers were scattered around the computer. The assignment was to write a series of 'shorts' looking at an incident, mundane or extraordinary (our choice), from several perspectives, each written in the first person and to be no longer than 300 words. It's a module from the creative writing degree course I'm on at university. Many now-famous writers have passed through this same course. I've waited a lifetime for the opportunity but, now it's come, I'm not so sure. I used to concentrate intently—narrative, tension and plot (which reminds me of something my little nephew, Niall, said to me last Bonfire Night: gunpowder, treacle and sponge). But you listen and get ever more confused until writing feels mechanical, maths with letters instead of numbers. The lecturers make something natural and easy seem complex, so that afterwards your writing is so forced and thought-about it becomes mere simulation, a body with no heart. It's probably best to let what they tell you buzz around like mad light and make sense of it later when it settles, except this is difficult when much of their advice is contradictory. The hope, maybe, is that you'll go through it all and come back to what you were, only more sure of yourself—that's if you've not been scared off completely which is okay because at least you can then get on with life again, cut loose from those burning dreams that you might count for something and commemorate your existence by having your name on a book.

I first had doubts a few weeks into the course. We had an outing to the pub, students and lecturers. We were tipsy, dispersed in small groups through several busy, wood panelled rooms. I remember thinking how different the atmosphere was from pubs back home. The chatter and body language was easy; a standoff or fight wasn't going to break out at any moment. In my circle, we were telling each other of the books we planned to write. I said mine would feature normal, everyday people because I knew them well, all along my street and round the block. These characters would be out-in-the-rain types, I said, huddled at bus stops or meandering through neighbourhoods, a bit lost. They'd sift for bargains at the second-hand market in town. They'd watch telly—quiz shows, soaps and those confessional programmes where people take lie detector tests (while the crowd boos or cheers) to prove they did (or didn't) have sex with their stepdaughter or sister-in-law from a previous marriage. I finished my little speech by declaring that I would give 'the mundane its beautiful due'. A few did comedy groans but they mostly nodded and smiled. About ten minutes later, when the group had thinned out, Andrew, one of the youngish lecturers, came over, eyes lit dark. He was drinking sips of orange cordial from a pint pot.

"I was listening to what you were saying before," he said.

"I was kind of joking."

"Fine, I guessed that but I was going to say that in principle anything that lends authenticity to your writing has to be a good thing. The problem with subject matter literally so close to home is a tendency to romanticise. And, probably more importantly, people generally don't want to read about the prosaic. They want the extraordinary or, if not, the ordinary underpinned with tension, the sense that something is about to happen."

Walking back to the halls of residence that night, light on my feet, head woozy, I wondered how anyone could speak as Andrew had done, so definitively. Does anyone really know what people want? Isn't all success merely good luck or great timing later formed into a rationale or shaped into formula so it can be held up, celebrated, copied? I remember looking at the stars. I was lonely, missing Sarah and home.

The hum of the computer fan was irritating, the bland perpetualness of the bloody thing. And I couldn't think of a single incident, mundane or extraordinary, that I wanted to write about. Who thinks of these modules, anyway? Is that the best they can do? I turned off the computer and a richer better silence flooded the room, and my mind.

Saturday

Sarah turned up wearing a cream-coloured coat and brown suede boots. I don't think I'd ever seen her looking so pretty. We went to a stately house, a National Trust pile. We often joked that we much preferred coffee and cake in a dusty café or a steak and ale pie in a country pub to a night out clubbing and drinking. 'We're like two pensioners,' she'd say. I'd counter that it was merely a received but specious 'wisdom' that everyone in their twenties spent their time high on drugs, smashed on alcohol, fornicating in the toilets at nightclubs where they played the same boom-boom-boom House track, ad nauseam. 'See, only a pensioner would talk like that,' she'd laugh.

Amid the mahogany panelling and shadowy corners, and with the 500 year old floorboards creaking beneath our feet, I felt unusually at peace with myself. Sarah was cheerful, trying to get me interested in everything: the glass case containing Victorian dentistry tools; sepia photographs from China; watercolours of tea parties and men fishing by a river, painted by artists called Walter, Edgar, Alec or George.

Afterwards we walked in the grounds. She stopped in front of an ornamental lake, gorse bushes in timid bloom at the bank and the bony silhouette of birch trees reflected on the water—without leaves, not yet trusting to a summer-to-come. It was early afternoon but with only us around for a minute or two, it had the fresh feeling of a new morning. The light on her hair was soft and white. She leaned against a metal fence and, peering into the image at the back of my digital camera, I saw her smile: open, trusting, alive. I caught it. Click, there it was. Everything about the picture was perfect. I know you can see anything you want in a photograph but if you showed it to anyone and asked what they thought, they'd say that the girl was in love with the photographer, easy.

As we strolled she reached for my hand a few times and her squeezing it was like she was rinsing out my heart, getting rid of some of the badness. In the half-light beneath the trees, padding down gently on the gravel path, it felt that being among all this beauty and quiet I could form a clear head, a new start.

Joe is the designated mentor of my study group. He is the lecturer who is expected to provide what was described in the university handbook as 'pastoral' care. He's a thickset bloke; it looks as if it would take a while to walk all the way around him. Minutes into his first lecture he told us of his hatred of Alan Sinclair, the university vice-chancellor. He spoke with a bluntness that was shocking at the time but to which we've become accustomed. He called Sinclair an arsehole, specifically a mealy-mouthed, self-obsessed, career-fixated and gutless arsehole. We were new to the university, new to each other, new to Joe—what did we care of the man who was running the place and how he went about it? The few who had seen Sinclair described an apparently benign figure with grey hair, half moon glasses, usually clad in corduroy trousers and chunky knit sweaters. They said it was hard to imagine him rousing much emotion but it seemed this very blandness had Joe frothing at the mouth, frequently.

On the drive back from the stately home Sarah began talking about her job. She worked in an office where they processed grant applications. The staff mixed with theatre and art groups, advising them how to market themselves and increase 'footfall'—I hate that word. She always talks about her colleagues as if I know them, as if everyone in the world knows them. Ben is the dark-haired lad. Goes out with Emma. You know, blonde hair, wears a lot of make-up. Jody's mad. Will do anything for a laugh: Mad Jody. Mr King's the boss, Matthew King. Okay enough. Bit of a stickler. Can have a real laugh with him when he's in the mood. At last year's Christmas party he put tinsel around his neck and made everyone sing carols. Says he used to be a professional footballer but they can't find mention of him on the internet or in any of the record books.

I don't talk to Sarah about people *she* doesn't know. If it was important, someone dying or getting a book published, I'd mention them but not otherwise.

She said they had introduced a new rota and she was down to work on Christmas Eve.

"What they've done is let all those who've got kids have time off over Christmas. It's not fair," she said.

The muscles around her eyes tightened. Christmas was months away, I said.

"It'll be here sooner than you think. Why should they have it just because they've got kids? It was their choice to have them."

"I suppose you're right," I said.

I sneaked a look. Her lips were shut tight. She stared straight ahead as if aware of my looking and not wanting to shift the setting of her face. I grabbed her knee playfully.

"Come on, it's not the end of the world," I said.

"It matters, though."

"Have your say and see how things go."

"You'd be bothered if it was you."

"It is me, in a way. It will impact on my Christmas too if you're not around," I said.

"Not as much as it will impact on me."

I wasn't sure whether she was being sarcastic.

I've been having one-to-ones with Joe or 'appraisals' as they're called—a term he resents ('They're chats, why the need to formalise everything?'). He's a big one for honesty, telling it like it is, in life and in your writing. It's his thing. He doesn't care how you take it; it's coming all the same. One student, Abigail, handed in an assignment. He'd been cool about other work she'd done and she told a few of us that she suspected he didn't like her writing style. He made her read the latest piece aloud. It was autobiographical, about her parents rowing when she was about eleven years old, doors slamming through the house and her sitting on the settee in a nightie, arms around her knees. She'd picked out fine detail and was insightful and even a bit funny at the same time but with no tricks going on, just telling the story. Joe said it was mediocre. He said the word so dismissively that you had to check it wasn't spelt, s.h.i.t. He might have been making a stand, setting down a benchmark we were each expected to achieve. After the 'mediocre' put-down he said (and this was during the first few weeks when I was ultra keen, recording lectures, so I had it down verbatim):

"Some day, Abi, there'll be a story you want to tell for no better reason than because it matters to you more than any other. You'll stop looking over your shoulder to make sure you're keeping everybody else happy, and you'll simply write what's real and true. Honest writing always makes people nervous, and they'll think of all kinds of ways to make your life hell. One day a long time from now you'll cease to care anymore who you please or what anybody has to say about you. That's when you'll finally produce the work you're capable of."

He hardly knew her at the time and probably still doesn't, to be so sure what she was all about and where she would end up.

I watched the road, recalling Sarah's face in the picture an hour or so earlier and thinking how quickly a mood could set in. I tried to remember whether she had always been this way. Perhaps, back in the early days of me and her, the crabbiness was barely discernible and I might even have considered it cutesy and easily repelled.

She liked to talk but she was also a pretty good listener. I think she liked me best when I was theorising, setting ideas free, opening up. I sometimes sensed her watching my lips and a look often came upon her as if she had fallen under an incantation, though I might be flattering myself; it's hard to

14

tell. Perhaps this was the difference between us—she seldom spoke in that intensely analytical way. She'd stop me short, snapping me back to earth: 'Well said, but who's going to buy the next drink?' I'm not sure when it began to fall heavier, the mood. Was I responsible? Did something about me or the way I acted, things I said, bring it on?

Another of Joe's discourses was his 'stark bollock naked' theory. At least this was funny. He said he believed that a writer's commitment to honesty and bravery was unconditional. For example, you're wandering naked through your hometown. A timid writer would, he said, cover himself up, a hand placed over his metaphorical nuts. But no, you're supposed to walk through there, past the municipal gardens and the town hall, showing everyone what you've got. I knew what he meant with all this but, as he spoke, I was thinking how he'd love the attention. Big flabby dick in the wind. Picture in the local paper (from the waist up). Really, it wasn't honesty he was expounding but exhibitionism, which was a different thing entirely.

We've all read Joe's books. He more or less insisted, telling us to look upon it as research, a 'vital and necessary addendum to his lectures'. They were published years ago, back in the early 1980s or thereabouts, and are quite hard to track down. The same photo is on the back cover of most of them, him scowling in front of a brick wall, nibbling at his lips. It's easy to discern what his expression is saying: 'Don't expect a gentle joyous tale, dear reader. Fuck that! I'm coming to get you and assail your sensibilities. I'm here to stir up within you irritation, anger, self-doubt and moral ambiguity'. How kind of him to put his picture on there, getting his mate out with a decent camera on a white-edged winter afternoon. When authors do this, you don't have to inconvenience yourself reading the first page to try them out. You can tell by the photo whether you're going to like their work or not, every time.

I drove in silence and wondered whether I was sulking or if it was a natural consequence to become quiet when someone was being unreasonable. She had been unreasonable, hadn't she, implying I didn't care about her having to work at Christmas? I'm not good at knowing how to gauge these things, or react. I have an instinctive response, I quickly rationalise and soften it and usually go back, more or less, to the first but it is now without heat or sting and I feel as if I'm letting myself down, compromising, selling myself short. Or, alternatively, that I am brooding unnecessarily, making too big a deal of everything. So then I'm confused. Afterwards I even worry about this confusion and it leads to a kind of low level stress that never goes away, which is my life.

It's strange. You meet someone like Joe, outsized but otherwise fairly ordinary looking but you haven't got a clue unless you read the book, which is the equivalent of an X-ray of their soul to hold against the light, or, in his case, the dark. On page 91 of *The Aftermath* a bloke jerks off into a high-heel shoe, his girlfriend licks it off. Page 109: a woman puts clothes pegs on her nipples 'because only resolute and specific pain can ameliorate the ennui of existence'. Towards the end of the novel, the protagonist meets a 'hooker' and unfastens her bra. Joe writes: 'Released from their support, her breasts drooped like hanged men'. It's like this all the way through his work, so, despite yourself, you end up hunting down the dirty bits.

Another thing with him is the physiological detail and the places where he chooses to linger, to gorge. In his first novel there is an unpleasant scene that lasts nearly three pages featuring blood, shit, sweat, semen, the lot. He asked me about it in one of the seminars. I told him I wasn't sure it worked, this blood-shit-sweat-semen section, whether it contributed to the story. He didn't say but I knew he was thinking I was prudish. This is what they do, people like him. It's *your* problem. Not that he's peculiar or monumentally indulgent, of course. Why is he telling us this stuff anyway? Has something gone on somewhere that's done this to him and he believes telling us about it, writing it down, will get it further away from him? And, another thing, what was it with the publishing world back then, all that out-there stuff?

The quiet in the car was unbearable so I jabbed at the radio button. The news came on. A few weeks earlier a group of illegal Chinese immigrants had drowned in Morecambe Bay after being caught out by the tide while picking cockles. The newsreader said legal action would be taken against the gang masters who had organised the work team.

"Do you know what the local cockle pickers did when they saw what the Chinese were doing?" I asked Sarah.

She shrugged.

"They pointed at their watches and tried to warn them that the tide was coming in and they should return to land. Don't you think that was really good of them?"

"Wouldn't anyone do the same?" she asked.

"I'm not sure. I suppose there are only so many cockles to pick and if the Chinese were being paid next to nothing it must have affected the market value."

"I think it's sad all round," she said, before announcing suddenly:

"I told my mum I might go shopping with her today."

She hadn't mentioned this before. I looked at the time on the dashboard.

"It's a bit late."

"Not really."

Sarah had previously been the girlfriend of one of my best friends, Dan. We're not friends anymore. They had been in a relationship for about a year. He was ill the night we got together, in bed with stomach pains; he guessed it was a rumbling appendix. She'd spent most of that day nursing him. He said she needed a break and as good as insisted she went out with me and three or four others from our little gang which later dispersed when we went off to university. We visited a few bars and friends drifted away through the evening. I recall wishing this to happen, delighted at every goodbye. We were the last two. I said I'd walk her home. It was late August. The day had been warm but darkness brought a chill.

"Want to borrow my jacket?"

(I didn't realise this was a staple of films and a precursor to exactly what happened soon afterwards, our coming together.)

"Yes, please."

It was too big for her. She looked sweet in all that denim. She smiled. I wanted her so much. I had wanted her for weeks, months. Thinking about her at night, unable to sleep, then waking to daylight and heartbreak, realising anew that she was someone else's. I had imagined her kiss, her undressing, her touch and the talking, one-on-one about everything that properly mattered. Sometimes in company she had made remarks so funny or incisive that I wanted to clasp her to me regardless of the consequences. She'd proffer an opinion—big or small, important or trivial—and it felt as if she was speaking my thoughts, except without self-consciousness or my need to qualify or show off. She just said it, plainly and brilliantly, and I soon became aware that I often volunteered, 'That was what I was thinking' or found myself nodding and smiling, perhaps too visibly happy to have found this more succinct other self. Her being with Dan had grown ever more painful. Sure, I told myself, he had asked her out and been rewarded with a yes but theirs was like a friendship formed on the first day of a new term, slightly forced and awkward and destined to be transient. But me and her was destined. We fitted. Matched up. Had to be.

That night, we walked past brightly lit Indian takeaways; taxi ranks; car parks; the shutdown dairy and the huge mill that looked like a docked battleship, now converted to flats. On the edge of town we came to derelict buildings where pigeons cooed inside. Wickets and wobbly goal posts were chalked on a school wall. We passed houses with curtains drawn; I thought of kids a similar age to Niall, asleep in their bedrooms. Cars drifted by, one then another. It was getting late. Within minutes of us being alone together I had noticed that there was hardly a need to finish sentences—we each knew the point that was being made, understood it. She got every joke and every nuance of what I was saying, and me her. I asked how many books she'd read.

"Not a lot. I don't need to. I'm one of those people who knows."

"Knows?"

"I know people, what they're thinking, how it all fits together. Life, the universe. You go and read your million books and you might catch me up one day in the brain department."

"Show off!"

"How can it be showing off, when it's the truth?"

She stopped and looked into my face, grinning.

"You're not the only brain box in the world," she said.

I'd known a little of her background through Dan but, while we walked, she told me much more about herself. Her parents had met quite late in life when they were working for the council. Sarah was an only child. Her mother had twice miscarried.

"Was that before or after they had you?"

"No one's ever asked me that," she said. "It was before, actually. Mum told me she was very lucky to have a kid at her age and it was God's way."

20

"What are they like, your parents?" I asked.

"My mum's really cheerful."

"And your dad?"

She laughed.

"He's never happier than when he's moaning!"

She said both her parents went to church each week and helped out with the collection, organised the flowers, raised money for missions to Africa.

"I used to go when I was little but not so much these days," she said. "I like the people there but most of all it's the quiet. I love being in public places when it falls really, really quiet. It feels special."

I knew that feeling.

"I'd go to church just to smell the burning candlewax," I said.

"And whatever that polish is that they use on pews. I could sniff that all day," she said.

We came to a pub and peered inside. The lights were off, towels draped over beer taps.

"That's a public place, gone quiet," I said.

"Not quite the same thing, but close."

We moved on and came to an alley near to where she lived. I kept her talking.

"Good night."

"Good night."

"Come here a second," I said.

"Why?"

"I want to kiss you."

It was a strong kiss, my lips pressed tight to hers. I ran my fingers through her hair. All this didn't feel like me, the me I'd known all my life until that point. It was borrowed—the boldness, the belief in myself and the moment. I imagined it would have to go back in the morning and I might never have it again. We parted and I'm not sure why but I ran home, sprinting down the canal bank. I felt odd as if I'd given in to growing up, holding and kissing a girl. I was happy to burst but then full of remorse, thinking of Dan. Sarah blamed me later, saying I shouldn't have walked her home, shouldn't have kissed her. I said she shouldn't have let me, shouldn't have borrowed my jacket.

She finished with Dan a few days afterwards, not telling him about me, just that she didn't love him anymore, simple. She was eighteen.

"I've done it," she said.

"Was he okay?"

"A bit upset."

She might have said the next bit to make me feel better:

"We'd not been getting along as well as we used to anyway."

I was impressed by her strength of character. Straight to the point: 'I don't love you any more'. I don't think I could ever do that to someone I'd once loved. I'd skirt around, dally for a while, making sure they were okay, letting them have slowed down pain rather than a sudden killing stab.

It must be love (for me), I thought, to make her so sure and clearheaded and ruthless when she was habitually such a compassionate and caring person. I did wonder, for a second (no more): would I one day receive this same cool brush off?

No, it was driven by an overwhelming need to be with me, a once in a lifetime episode of emotional brutality, an obligatory piece of business borne from high love.

Sarah was adamant about an early-evening shopping trip with her mum.

"Are the shops open now?" I asked. "I know supermarkets are but, you know, clothes shops and that?"

"Of course they are. It's Saturday."

I dropped her off at her parents' and, peering at the sky, realised there was enough daylight left to make it worthwhile taking out Niall. It didn't have to be anywhere specific with him. We'd usually end up at a patch of countryside fairly close to home. On your own, you drive past these tracts of land down little-known roads between houses and buildings but with a kid by your side they become tiny kingdoms where you're soon snapping through branches, smelling damp earth or lying down among bracken. We always find things, too: bird feathers, frog skeletons, weird shaped sticks, rocks covered in moss, ferns that double as swords. Niall likes to pick up bugs and watch them flip and crawl on his palms. We dam streams and catch tiny fish in nets. Last autumn we collected blackberries and those we didn't eat we squeezed so we could daub the sticky juice on his face and call it warpaint. It's great that there aren't any rules. He can fall over, pick things up, toy fight with me in the tall grass. Jenny (his mum, my sister) is usually too whacked out for all this. She wants time to herself, to stay in and read the paper, watch television and have a rest. She needs it after all the worry.

When we first got together Sarah was so without guile that she invited confession. She had what I hadn't, or at least she appeared to—she was comfortable in her skin, not pushing and shoving and tense, not overthinking all the time. She could sit by the fire all day, reading, listening to the radio or the rain, stirring only when she had to. I imagined she was attracted to my energy, the doing, but she might not have been; she's never said what she likes about me. I'm not as well versed as Loachy but I'm not sure girls *do* tell you, not in much detail. I think you're meant to know intuitively through a kiss or a smile or because they phone or text you regularly and want to see you.

Early on, I told her about other girls I knew, those I liked or disliked. I joked that her legs were thin, that she was skinny all over. Perhaps I should have said beautifully skinny, made it more of a compliment or, better still, not even made the comment. You've got to be very careful what you say. Girls are clever. They shrug or smile but it goes in deep. It might be weeks, months or even years before they mention it again. They always remember.

We kept our relationship secret at first. Let the dust settle, the world turn. Neither of us wanted Dan to know what we'd done, especially me. Every few days I'd meet Sarah at a bar on the other side of town.

"You seem fed up," she'd say as we sipped our drinks.

I'd nod but not answer. I resented what she'd done: leaving

someone so callously, as good as breaking him in half (I had engineered, with great care, to barely see him but the bulletins from friends were not good. He was devastated.).

"But I did it to be with you."

I'd put my arms around her and draw her close.

"I know, I'm sorry."

But I was the same the next time, every time, blaming her for Dan's misery and knowing that doing this made her reiterate her love for me. Do you love me? Yes. Can I hear that again? Can I hear it every minute of every day? I was seeking the love parents gave: unconditional, perpetual. Sarah didn't need this—a cruel, vindictive new boyfriend, seeping insecurity and weakness, too cowardly to take his share of responsibility. That said, she had finished with him rather efficiently.

While we were still so new to love, it fighting for light, I kept thinking of what made a relationship break down. Did all your slyness, peevishness and sneaky little tricks accumulate until your partner's internal dial moved incrementally from devotion to toleration to indifference to dislike? Or did it merely change one catastrophic day—love move on? That was how it must have seemed to Dan. He'd done nothing wrong. He couldn't have loved her more. Sending her out that evening while he was ill was symbolic of his selflessness and trust. If he'd asked her to stay, they might still be together. A good deed brought upon him such loss. Love gone. Life changed. And there we were, Sarah and me, loving and then fighting, sure and then doubting, while he was fastened to his bed (the stomach ache superseded by lovesickness).

I even contrived to be jealous of Dan, peeved that he had

got there first. I wanted to own Sarah's past and present, to be everything to her, before and always.

"How was I to know that you fancied me when I was with him?" she asked.

Couldn't you tell? Didn't you feel what I did? The way our personalities locked together. The bliss of being alone for those few moments when Dan left a room. Those looks between us. How could you not know? I pushed it relentlessly, crueller than cruel.

"Look," she shouted (eventually). "He means nothing to me. It's over. Why do you keep going on about the past?"

On to the next enigma: if she had loved him once, how could he now mean so little to her? She had gone from seeing him, loving him almost every day, to not even texting or phoning to check on his wellbeing. Was it so easy to move her heart from one person to another?

"You're stupid, you, the way you twist things," she yelled. "We've only just got together and you're driving us apart. I left him because I love you. It's you I want to be with. I wasn't going to stay with him out of sympathy. I liked him too much for that. Don't you understand?"

Although unacknowledged, Jenny knows I make a fuss over Niall partly because I'm afraid he won't be around forever. It hurts to even write that down, as if I'm tempting fate. I know all this superstition stuff is rubbish but it's hard to let go. Some days I think if I stop believing he's going to be okay, he'll become sicker and it will be my fault because I forgot to hope. It's always been part of my family, rituals such as wearing green for good luck; touching wood; never crossing on the stairs; saying 'rabbit' on the first day of a new month; and, of course, keeping umbrellas closed indoors. These are all vaguely comical but I was also led to believe it was a folly to assume good things would happen to you and, worse, evidence of conceit. Life was presented as a sadistic game of hopscotch. Land on the wrong number and, boy, you'd pay. The odds were never discussed, only the consequences, the retribution. Happiness or sorrow and everything in between had to be moderated otherwise God (an ill-defined superior being) would hear you laughing or crying and begin his games. You might bring illness upon yourself, humiliation, failure—this meant anything you wanted or hoped might happen had to be acquired through a paradigm of wishing but not wishing, supplication and gratitude, thoughts crisscrossing endlessly.

Niall being ill was a dilemma. No one was quite sure how we'd brought it upon ourselves and why a kid was suffering for something we'd possibly done or not done. And how come, with all our aggregated powers, we'd not been able to will him to good health?

It took about a year before the shadow of Dan was finally chased away. There was one particular Saturday afternoon when I realised how much I'd fallen in love with Sarah. We were visiting friends who had hired a cottage in the Lake District. Everyone but us two had gone out. I was sitting on a windowsill while Sarah watched an old film on television.

Outside, the sky was blue and black and the buildings and hills were merging in a darkness pocked by occasional smudges of amber streetlights. She'd made a pot of coffee and we sipped from mugs. I realised I'd never felt like this before, as if she was all around and I was breathing her in. I watched her from the side, the hair on her shoulders, the light splashing her face as the television flickered. Being near her, with her, felt to be everything.

The summer afterwards we went on holiday together and I had that intensity of feeling again. I drove the car with the windows open most of the way, elbows in the breeze. When we arrived at the seaside it was one of those rare English days of total stillness, the heat fierce. We found a park. She lay on her back in the grass. She was wearing a loose floral blouse and her skin was turning honey-coloured in the sun. Freckles appeared at the centre of her neck. The grass was sappy and I pulled at a few strands, squeezing them in my hand to leave a trace of green. I stroked a blade across her forehead. I tracked down from her neck to where her breasts lay flat against the rib cage beneath the cotton. I leaned to kiss her lips. She jerked forwards, startled, and there was briefly an expression of pique until a soft smile fell over her face. She wanted to move on and gathered up her bag.

"It's too hot here."

As we walked away she reached for my hand and gripped it tight. Her hand was warm and small and without thinking I lifted it in mine and kissed it hard across the knuckles. We strolled around the shops close to the harbour. She wanted to buy postcards and write home.

Later we drove a mile or so to a holiday park with a wooden sign hanging from a gate showing that it had vacancies. A narrow dirt road led to a knot of chalets enclosed by privet hedges. One was marked 'Office' with a compound by its side holding dozens of gas bottles. I left the car and knocked on the door. No answer. I walked inside. The sun-fired air smelled of woodiness and creosote. Dust danced in wide arcs of light from the windows. After a few seconds the door opened behind me. A man entered wearing overalls. He rummaged for his glasses on the desk, through grubby oil-scuffed pieces of paper. He gave me the key to a chalet and said it was fine to pay tomorrow when we were leaving.

"You've got an honest face," he said.

After we'd unpacked, we tipped white wine into enamel mugs and lay on the bed in the chalet. The sun was going down, the light fading. I inserted into the Alba one of a number of compilation CDs I'd burned especially for the holiday. The song opened with strummed chords on an acoustic guitar. Lying on the bed, our bodies parallel to each other, we held hands at our side to form the shape of an 'M'. The singing began:

> *'When there's things to do not because you gotta,*
> *when you run for love not because you oughta,*
> *when you trust your friends with no reason notta,*
> *the joy I've named shall not be tamed,*
> *and that summer feeling is gonna haunt you*
> *one day in your life.'*

We didn't speak or move while the song played. It was our day set to music, summer in a song.

"Who's it by?" she asked as it faded.

"Jonathan Richman. He's one of my dad's favourite singers."

"It's beautiful," she said.

I think we were most in love at that time.

When I got to Jenny's she was playing toy soldiers with Niall on the kitchen table. She looked pleased to see me. Niall had some news:

"A man's gone purple in a town hall," he said. "On his head."

Jenny explained:

"He's just seen it on the telly. Tony Blair has been pelted with purple powder by one of those Fathers 4 Justice protestors at the House of Commons."

"Is he all right?"

"Apart from turning purple, he's fine."

We'd grown close since she'd had Niall. I didn't feel like her kid brother anymore, but more a friend. Babies, waiting for them to come, arriving, caring for them, it reminds you that you're family, all in it together.

You can't tell Niall is ill; it doesn't really show. And we're not sure what's actually wrong with him anyway, except that it's possibly quite serious. He's always having tests at the hospital. They say it might be his glands or his blood. Some days he's tired but all kids get like that. He hangs on to your clothes, wanting to be picked up, or he'll curl up on the settee, thrashing about. Mum calls it rangy. He always seems to be worse in the house, so that's why I try to get him outdoors. The fresh air and freedom gets him giggling and running, jumping. 'Like a frog', he croaks.

I have a photo of Niall on my bedroom wall. He's in a field of tall grass, arms flapped out and forearms facing upwards as if carrying an invisible tray. He's wearing a smile that makes his cheeks swell and his eyes almost disappear in the creases. Loachy said it looked a bit sinister, Children of the Corn and all that. He once asked if he could paint a portrait of Niall. I thought: how come you've hardly ever painted any other kids? Admit it, it's because you think he's going to die, isn't it? *I* was allowed to think this, possibly, as his uncle, but it felt vulgar coming from him. And if he did paint him he'd probably make him look odd, all waxy-eyed and half way to gone; that's his style. He did a picture of me a few years ago and I looked weird, head too big for my body, little skinny arms. I asked if that was how he saw me and he said he did, pleased with himself.

"How do you see yourself, man?" he asked.

"Better looking than that."

He asked, smirking, if my vanity had been affronted. This often happened, he said, people imagining they were better looking than they were. He pitied them. I should have said that I felt sorry for him, uglifying people and smirking about it.

*

31

Jenny's boyfriend, Simon, had been away most of the time she was pregnant. And now he's gone for good. He was an environmental activist, out to save the world from global warming, deforestation, famine, pollution and any other causes you could think of that were righteous and vital and involved meetings and petitions and campaigns and leaflets and marches and badges. He didn't do chitchat but sermonised, using his hands, fidgeting. He had a great sense of urgency as if he believed time was running out and he'd like to atomise himself so he could simultaneously be up a tree protesting about a bypass being built; on a Greenpeace ship blockading a whaling fleet or firing off hundreds of e-mails to newspapers.

He was distinctly uncomfortable around any kind of luxury and unable to focus on what he considered peripheral, such as family life, which is why he'd more or less disowned his brothers and sisters, mum and dad. He had a peculiar view of children, too—they were fundamentally evidence of ego and self-love. He believed it was best if children were reared communally.

He gave me a lift once in his car that smelled of wet soil and appeared to be held together by parcel tape. He was very patient, explaining why Castro had been important as a figurehead of defiance to the United States and how Marcus Garvey had served the same function for the Jamaican people. He cracked a few jokes and, although I was only a kid then, I recognised his smart, dry humour. He also took mum off, putting on her throaty, exasperated voice, berating him for being a vegetarian.

It was an open secret that he had another girlfriend, several possibly, in London or thereabouts. Jenny didn't seem to mind, having a part-share appeared to suffice.

"He's taking the bloody mickey," mum said. "Who is he anyway? Hardly God's gift to womankind."

(When Simon first came to the house mum must have thought he was a passing fancy because she announced after he'd left, within earshot of Jenny, that he was a 'funny-looking bugger'. He was a very slight man with tiny hands and skin so pale it was almost transparent.)

Jenny, to bait mum, said he believed in free love, people being allowed to express themselves physically with whom they chose, when they chose.

"Well, why don't you express yourself with some other bloke? See how he likes that."

"He'd be happy for me," she said.

"Happy, my eye. He'd go up the wall and if he didn't, there'd be something wrong with him."

"I'm not sure, mum. He's not like anyone you've ever come across before."

"Give over, he's read a few daft ideas in a book and got carried away with himself."

I'd hardly had a sip of tea when Niall put his face close to mine.

"Are we going on this walk or anything?" he asked.

"Niall, with that smile we'll walk at least a mile."

"Is that a proper poem, from a book?"

"Could be."

"Shall I get my wellies?"

"Get thems wellies," I ordered.

Jenny lived with Niall in the same place where she'd been with Simon a few years before, a small rented house on a main road where the ornaments (wooden dolphins, brass Buddhas, wind chimes) shook when lorries trundled past. Whenever I called round back then, usually on my way home from school, Simon would be loading stuff into his car or dashing to the railway station.

"Got a meeting to go to, can't stop. Jenn, hurry up with those posters."

Maybe Jenny liked this best about him. She'd found someone who wasn't inert like most of the rest of the people in the neighbourhood; he knew the routes out of town. She was also surprisingly otherworldly considering the pragmatism painted onto us by our parents and the rest of the family. Almost as soon as we could speak or at least understand, they were feeding us the cold porridge of realism, keeping us in our place, pointing out the folly of dreaming. It was nothing personal or, indeed, intentional; it came as natural as their next breath. There were limits to Jenny's complaisance with Simon, though. She insisted he had been there when Niall was born.

She often spoke to me in great detail about the birth as if she believed that whatever was wrong with Niall began there and by raking through her memory she might find a clue that could help her better understand his condition. The contractions had started during a downpour. Jenny said they were drenched in seconds, rushing to the car. It was windy too, streetlights sending out jolts of jittery light and garden fences banging against concrete posts. She was anxious. She'd had an earlier miscarriage. After several hours at the hospital she asked to go into the birthing pool. Simon liked this coalition with nature. As she lowered herself in she said her mood changed drastically. Simon was stroking her back, trying to soothe her but causing great irritation.

"Why was that?" I asked.

"Because I knew he had an agenda. Even then, at a time like that. He was thinking how great it was to have a natural birth in water but he had no idea how much pain I was in. No idea."

She told me she had asked Simon whether she should take the pain relief being offered. Instead of answering properly he kept saying, 'If you think that's best.'

Pethidine had little effect. She was offered gas and air. She devoured it, keeping the mask to her face, in love with the drowsiness. The midwives said a Ventouse delivery was necessary. Fierce lights were switched on, her feet placed in stirrups. A rubber sucker was placed inside Jenny on to the baby's head. Finally, nearly a full day after her waters had broken, Niall was born. He had a large purple patch at the crown of his head where the sucker had burst blood vessels. He cried through the night, the next day and most of the days afterwards.

"He's not had an easy birth," the midwives said. "He'll settle. Imagine if you'd been pulled out of a small dark hole by your head. He's got a thumping headache."

*

We drove a mile or two out of town, past the ice cream van in the lay-by close to the reservoir. The Polish girl was leaning glumly on the counter. She recognised us from previous visits and shouted as I parked up:

"Not long now before I go home. Last chance for ice cream or ice lolly."

"We'll have one next time," I said.

"Up to you," she said and repositioned her elbows at the serving hatch.

Niall wanted to play 'Gulliver'. We tripped down a footpath for a few hundred yards, turning into a broad patch of fern. He made me sit on the ground with him. At this level the stems were like miniature trees. I had to make up stories about the imaginary people all around us, so small that they could barely be seen. He collected woodlice and bugs, herding them into a compound he'd made from tiny twigs.

"This is a farm and I'm the farmer," he said.

"And who am I?"

"You're just a man."

"Can I be one of the people who helps at the farm?"

"Not really. You sit there and I'll be telling you what to do."

"Okay."

The day after Niall had been born we all made our way to the hospital and formed a horseshoe shape around the bed: mum, dad, nan, Simon and his parents. Jenny's eyes were heavy. Dried blood was on her nightie. While we were there Niall had his picture taken. The hospital photographer shuffled into the ward with a bag full of equipment and a Winnie the Pooh toy to coax a smile: Baby's First Photo. Niall was bawling. The tears made his skin glossy as if he'd been varnished specially for the occasion. The picture is now on the mantelpiece at mum's, on the wall at Jenny's, in my wallet.

Niall was passed among us, still crying. He's got his mum's eyes, his dad's nose, we said. Simon held him limply. He might have been nervous because mum was watching; she sometimes had that effect. Simon's mum had a cardigan folded over her knee. His parents were much older than ours. They didn't say much. Thinking back now, I'm surprised they were there considering Simon's anti-family stance. Dad asked if they wanted to go back to our house for a drink to 'wet the nipper's head'. They said they needed to head home before the roads got too busy.

We played among the ferns for about an hour until Niall grew bored. He began kicking out at his mini farm, saying the baddies had come and were very, very angry. He was quiet in the car on the way back. I asked what he was thinking.

"You're not meant to ask little boys questions like that."

I smiled.

"You're right," I said. "Three cheers for the clever little bugger."

"And you're not meant to swear."

While in hospital Jenny asked the nurses and doctors continually if Niall was all right, whether it was normal to cry so much.

The earlier miscarriage and the long labour was on her mind. She'd been ill while pregnant too and had spent time in hospital with stomach pains and bleeding. Mum had no doubt:

"Something's wrong with him. Why can't they do anything? Babies don't cry and cry like that for no reason. Look at him, he's in agony. All the things they're supposed to have in hospitals these days, the advances they've made in medicine."

Simon left Jenny within a week of Niall being born. He told her he knew fully the magnitude of the decision but had made it because he didn't want to be disingenuous. He was too young for fatherhood, he said, there were things he wanted to do, causes to champion, places to see, people to meet. Mum said he should have thought about all that before; it wasn't as if he was sixteen years old. Hell, you were meant to know what you wanted by your mid-twenties. And what was he giving up? He still had his life. He made it sound as if having a kid was the same as dying, mum raged.

Jenny told us later that she'd been desperate for a baby—she wasn't sure why—and Simon, before she even fell pregnant, had made it clear that he wasn't prepared to 'commit to the binding and choking ties of the nuclear family'. She told me she always believed that, on seeing the baby, Simon would change his mind and his paternal instinct override his beliefs. She was wrong, it turns out, but saw no point in making him do something he didn't want to; she couldn't make him stay.

When they left hospital for home, Niall had to be next to Jenny all the time; he bawled if she put him down. The only way she could do housework was to strap him to her in a harness. He had to be kept occupied. Toys wouldn't suffice.

He had to be rocked, soothed, stroked. Once this stopped, he'd cry again as if his natural state was distress. In the evenings he raised his knees to his chest and the crying became interspersed with squalls of high-pitched shrieks. The health visitor said it was probably colic. I didn't know a baby's cry could hook into you like this, lifting you up and dangling you off the ground. It was heartbreaking. Jenny and mum more or less organised shifts to get through. Mercifully, he cried less when he began walking and trying to talk.

(For a while it angered me that Simon wasn't around to comfort my sister and their son. So many times I'd paced Jenny's front room singing and whispering to Niall, kissing him on the cheek, praying for him to fall calm, sometimes believing the cries might have been a plea for his dad to come back. Afterwards, I'd recognise that this wasn't fair. Simon being there wouldn't have stopped the crying. He didn't know Niall was a difficult baby and, later, a sickly child. As he saw it, he'd left Jenny with what she had wanted so much that a miscarriage and a disinclined partner hadn't deterred her. Also, hadn't I, and the rest of us, felt a strange and selfish euphoria when he first left? We could now have this baby as our own, belonging exclusively to our side of the family, one of us.)

While I was driving Niall back to Jenny's, a text came through on my Nokia. I saw it was from Sarah. Everything that had been on my mind fell from it instantly—Jenny, Simon, university, Loachy, even the little boy at my side squirming and pulling at his seatbelt. I felt shallow and stupid for prioritising this message above all else, letting it crash to the centre of my world. I pulled the car to the side of the road. The text said that she felt 'a bit ruff' and wasn't up to a 'Satdi nite out' (I'd learned long before not to conflate her irksome texting syntax with her personality). There was no 'X' in it, no declaration of love. I felt deflated. I drove off again. Niall tried to chat but I was distracted.

I dropped him off at Jenny's. She offered me a cup of tea but I declined. While I was standing in the front room I noticed how many reminders of Simon were still in the house: the porcelain phrenology head with a rasta hat plonked on top; a 'tree of life' poster pinned to the back of the door and a cluster of vintage button badges on the curtain—'Coal not Dole', 'Ban the Bomb', 'Whoever you vote for, the Government Wins' and 'Feed the Poor, Starve the Rich'. None of us had seen Simon since the day he left. He had said he didn't want to confuse Niall or give Jenny false hope (mum said she couldn't believe 'the arrogance of the little sod'). He didn't even collect his clothes from the house, telling her to pass them on to Oxfam. His only communication had come about four years after Niall was born when he sent Jenny a parcel tied with string. It contained a book and a postcard with a quote by Che Guevara printed in wonky letters on the front: 'Let me say, at the risk of sounding ridiculous, that the true revolutionary is guided by great feelings of love'. On the book's title page Simon had written, 'To Jenny and Niall, this is all I have to say, now and forever, Si'.

The 'book' (more a pamphlet, really) was a volume of

Simon's poetry titled *The Gutter of the Heavens Hangs Over Me* and was professionally produced with a photograph of a forest at nightfall on the cover. His own picture was on the back. His skin was even whiter than before, eyes pleading as if looking out from melting snow. The quote underneath was by someone called Christian Ranucci: 'This is a powerfully obsessive first collection; its dark imagery and unexpected juxtapositions are at the service of very real intelligence. Simon Bentley's poems speak to the gut as well as to the brain'.

I borrowed the book soon after it had arrived. I told Jenny that, as I was a writer-to-be, it held particular significance. One of the longer poems, The Delivery Room, was clearly about Niall. The protagonist (Simon, obviously) returns there after the birth to collect the mother's overnight bag (Jenny's, presumably). The bright lights are switched off now, replaced by an amber glow from a bedside lamp. He sees blood on the floor in 'syrupy dark red patches'. The bed sheets are drenched. A large metal dish is fastened to the foot of the bed and the placenta lies within it, purple and bloody like 'something you'd see in a butcher's shop window'. It closed with the line: 'It looked as if a murder had taken place in there, not a birth'.

Down the years I have picked through Simon's work many times. I wrote down the words that recurred, exposing, as I saw it, who he was and how he saw life. In the opening three poems he used black (four times), death or dead (three times), blood (twice), dark (twice), and one each of madness; stinking; sickened; fear and raped. I imagined Joe approving of such brackish prose. He liked the idea of us being among the suffered—the drinkers, the druggies, the prurient, the losers—viewing life as an ante room of hell. He saw a truth and majesty in it.

I asked Jenny if she planned to give the book to Niall when he was older.

"It might accidentally find its way into the bin before then," she said.

"Because it'll upset him?"

"No, because I don't want him to know his dad writes such bloody awful poetry."

I was proud to have a sister who could quote a Smiths lyric so nonchalantly.

Back at my parents', I tried to watch television but was restless, my head jammed tight with thoughts about Sarah, principally my reaction to her text—disproportionate excitement superseded by utter disappointment. That, and the overall mess of it all, what I'd got myself into. Why did I always overcomplicate everything? When you fall in love you're not supposed to question. You're meant to let go and see what happens. If you don't you could end up a grievous poet like Simon writing heavily allegorical stuff about a dying swan with a broken neck, covered in blood, on a stone, in the rain, under a tree, close to the raging sea.

But my form isn't good on these things. I question constantly. I fret. I check the pulse of my relationship with Sarah every few minutes. When I first fell in love with her I hadn't envisaged this wearisome and constant (on my part) power-play. I had no idea that I'd be stuck in a place (my head) with thoughts shouted at me: say this to her, don't say it, mention that, comment on this, look disinterested, be attentive, react, don't react, tell her your feelings, shut down, ask her what she's thinking, tell her you love her, don't tell her you love her, be compliant, be resistant, stick up for yourself, go along with it, praise her, criticise her, act modest, be bold, say something cheeky, say something profound, be more endearing, be more humdrum, tell her you can't make it tomorrow, tell her you can, let her have half the story, all of it, be hopeful, be pessimistic. This, I imagine, is what people do who can't trust that anyone would fall in love with them, the 'them' that is their true, natural self. When it does happen (and they ponder endlessly on why it has) they wait impatiently for the inevitable end, staring down the blackness, thinking always: any day now.

There's probably no need for all this with Sarah. She doesn't go in for mind games (if that's possible). For example, when I'm at university she phones or texts every night at six o'clock. Dead on. She doesn't keep me waiting to test me, see if I'm showing signs of hurting. And she's never early to catch me out or to appear extra keen. She doesn't ask that I call her either, to perhaps create a balance. Also, she doesn't tell me things to see how I react—things she might think I want to hear (flattery) or don't want to hear (criticism or how good-looking someone is, perhaps). All this has no effect, of course, doesn't pacify me one bit. The war in my head goes on.

Unlike her I *do* play mind games. It's what vulnerable people do: attack to defend. Hurting her in little bits, keeping the line between us stretched tight. How could you leave something like that to chance and trust that you were innately so likeable and lovable that it would go on forever, all this love?

There's no stopping these senseless games no matter how hard you really, really, God-help-me-please, want to be a sane and normal person. It's a disorder. You say things (blithely, obviously: 'Oh, there's this girl, she's really pretty') so you can check the look in her eyes, see if she cares enough to react. A solitary tear leaking down can make a happy day euphoric. In the end, though, when it comes to the end, I know none of this stuff will matter. She'll wake up one morning and merely decide she doesn't love me anymore.

Alone, Saturday night. From a distance of a few days away it can seem an agreeable idea. Read a book maybe, watch a film, enjoy the solitude and reflection burnished by other people's hubbub. But you have to be careful because if you don't meet the given time head-on and in the right mood, it can descend quickly, catch you unaware and become the loneliest and darkest few hours of the week. If you're falling, it's important that you don't look through a window where you might see people and cars and life passing by or, should you step outside, hear distant voices, laughter possibly. They are out there, the happy and the busy, joining together, lost to the moment. These same hours that stretch wide and empty before you are fast and fun for them, chased home with a smile, conversation or another drink.

I *was* falling, thinking how the whole thing with Kate

was typical, my scratchy thinking piled up into a catastrophe. I met her six months ago. I was trying myself out, how far I would go. Sarah had been indifferent to me, possibly. How do you tell? Properly tell? She'd been that way for a few days, maybe. Might have been a week or so. She went out with a few friends one night without asking me along. She said she'd invited me weeks before and I'd said I didn't want to go. A few days afterwards I asked if she fancied a trip to the seaside. She said she'd already arranged to see a workmate that day. She smiled as she told me. I wasn't sure if this signified an apology of sorts or was one of those looks that people give when imparting information you might not like: bet that hurt, didn't it? Everything is potentially symbolic when you're feeling down and anxious. I decided her choosing to spend a day with a friend instead of me was the mile wide signpost I'd been looking for. You want it this way ideally, big and clear, because you're not sure whether all the things that have got you to that state are significant or trivial. They're too often bitty, open to differing interpretations. You need something irrefutable, proof that she's falling out of love with you, losing respect and liking you less and less each passing week. And much as you'd want to, you can't tell her what you're feeling because then she'll realise how much you care. You're done for, truly and conclusively, if she realises she is the stronger and deserves better.

I stopped at three cans; I didn't want to wake up with a hangover.

Sunday

Almost as soon as I got out of bed, I texted Sarah:

'Any better?'

It was over an hour before she replied:

'Worse 2day. Throat sore, all shivery. Best not meet up. X'

At least I had an 'X' this time. I was ashamed. My mood, my day, come to this—dependent on whether she pressed a particular key on her phone. I needed to shake myself free of this craving and summon self-esteem, somehow. Perhaps it wasn't about finishing with Kate but the converse—I needed several girls to whom I could offer and receive fragments of love so that, should any desert me, the mosaic of me would still be visible, still strong. Then I thought how lucky I was with Kate, her being discreet and sane. In my absurd imaginary harem it would take only one of them to become mad with jealousy and spite and the lot would come down on me.

I wanted to clear my head. I phoned my mate Kizzy to see if he fancied a walk. As usual he took ages to answer and when he did it sounded as if it was the first time he'd spoken in years.

"Yeah, sounds a plan." he croaked. "Shall I ring Al?"

Al was Kizzy's best friend, though they were always falling out. I volunteered to drive and we headed to the hills on the outskirts of town, much further on from where I'd played with Niall the day before. I parked up and we followed a rough path. The mud was past our ankles in places. We ploughed on, heading to random landmarks—a tree, a ruin, the next hill. Eventually, four hours later, we were back where we'd started. Our cheeks were crimson, skin tingling and our bodies warmed up. Time for a rest, a bout of contemplation before we headed down the final hill to the car and civilisation. We sat on a rocky outcrop amid the coarse grass. Al and Kizzy put a match to little spitty hand-rolled fags, having quick puffs before the tips turned from red to black to dead. Within a few minutes of sitting down, the temperature felt to have dropped.

So, I became convinced Sarah was falling out of love. We'd disagreed a few times and I had the feeling I was annoying her by being me, the 'me' when I said things spontaneously, when I was relaxed. I'd even started wondering: were we that well matched anyway? She was irritating me a bit as well—all that talking about herself and people at work. And she often seemed to be at least half way to a sulk. The trivial stuff, too. Her new haircut was far too short. The way she opened her mouth when she applied lipstick was infuriating and her playing with her hair, twisting it between her fingers and the looking away sometimes when I spoke, making me search for eye contact. More than enough reasons. But this might have been a phase. It happens in all relationships. You're supposed to get through it. Don't do anything stupid. Wait for tomorrow. I'm not good at waiting. I decided, then: I'd show her what she was letting go, slipping through careless fingers. She's got this coming.

I went out with a mate from school I'd not seen for a

while. We drank all night, proper knocking it back, bar to bar, pint after pint. We met two girls in a nightclub. They were flirty, doing most of the talking. If she wants to be with me, I thought, this Kate girl, laughing, brushing against me, looking into my eyes, asking me to dance, asking about my life, pretty in a tight dress, smelling so good, well it's out of my hands. God's will. Happen happening. I've only got the one life; best make the most of it. Try everything, be everything. A goodnight kiss on the pavement. Phone numbers jabbed into our mobiles. No, let's not part now, standing out here among these drunken, rubbery people, the rain spitting down. We both knew where it was heading. We climbed into a taxi. Heavy kisses on the back seat. She's using her tongue. I want more. As much as I can get. Tomorrow never knows.

"You can go now—I'm staying," I told the taxi driver when he parked outside her house.

He winked at me. I resented his mateyness. The whole world was winking at me. I was in the scene for real now; the cheeky chappie had got lucky. We made love on the carpet in the living room. Sore knees. Condom tied in a knot afterwards, wrapped in a tissue and thrown into the pedal bin in the kitchen (past the potato peelings).

"Sssshh, don't wake my mum," she said.

"I'm more worried about your dad."

"He's dead."

"Oh, sorry."

She dressed quickly. Her face was flushed pink. She sat on the settee. She wanted to kiss, to be held. Okay, for a minute but then let me out of here, away from this house I don't know and this person I don't know who is clinging and staring at me with God knows what in her eyes. (I hope it's not lust because I'm done to death, empty.)

"Anyone fancy a drink?" asked Al.

He produced a flask of treacle black coffee. He had the sugar wrapped in a tiny piece of cellophane. They each had three spoonfuls per cup. Al drank silently. He had fallen morose now he was at the edge of a new week and set to return to his call centre job. He stood up and looked at the town below, shaking his leg to free the reedy grass stuck to his trousers. Street lights were coming on. The sky immediately above the roads and houses became a purple hue like a gas ring on a gigantic cooker. It was beautiful.

"It's shit here," said Al. "Wants a bloody bomb on it. What good's ever come out of it? Go on, tell me: one good thing."

Kizzy and me looked at one another. It wasn't that bad. And if you wanted to be pedantic you could name a few artists and actors, the odd musician. I didn't want to antagonise Al but Kizzy weighed in:

"Stop being a moaning bastard."

Al spun round, peeved. I pacified him:

"We'll go away soon, sort that trip out, hey?"

This had been discussed many times, almost as if having a plan, a dream of an escape, was enough in itself. I sensed that Al would have been happy to leave it this way once more but with the Sarah-Kate situation and the worry over

Niall, I was beginning to think we should actually do it, make it real.

"Count me out. I'm not going anywhere," said Kizzy.

After that first night and swearing, blood on forehead, that I wouldn't see her again, I phoned Kate. Even as we spoke I thought how pathetic and weak and desperate it felt, and exciting. That week, I came home from university specially to see her; it was supposed to be a study day. We went to a bar close to where she lived. I was the charmer: listening, laughing and looking deep into her eyes. She was wearing a pair of awful white jeans and too much foundation so her face was dry and powdery. She could really talk. You couldn't imagine commas or full stops in there, just a long drone in the same tone about what it was like in her office where they had to log the stuff that goes in and out of the warehouse and they have this computer program where they record import and export and she's been there for three years now and before that she worked in town for an accountant which was okay but not as good as the office above the warehouse because there wasn't as many girls her age and they weren't really up for a laugh. Suddenly, she said:

"You've got a girlfriend, haven't you?"

"Why do you say that?"

"I can tell a mile off. I'm not bothered. Well, I am, but I'm not if you know what I mean. Why aren't you with her tonight?"

"Because I'm with you." Had I really said that?

She looked at me fiercely. In that one look I saw her smartness lit poster bright. You could be snobby about her trousers, her job and the flaky, orangey make-up but she was astute, a seer. I kidded myself I had the third eye of the writer but she was ahead of me, round the block and back again before I'd even set off.

"I wanted to be with you again," I bleated. "I felt something on Saturday when I first spoke to you [did I? I'm not sure]. Things haven't been going well between me and my girlfriend [difficult to substantiate when one of the parties has sporadic but acute low self-esteem and a predilection to fatalism]."

I knew, sitting there trying to get fuzzy drunk, that there was no real justification for what I was doing. I was serving my ego, flattered that she wanted to spend time with me, have sex with me. She was an insurance policy, my possible next girlfriend. And it was all dimly related to an out-of-date ideal to which, at best, a quarter of me held dear. I wanted, as a writer, to get close to people quickly, suck in life, bathe in it, find out what it was like to step out of myself and, for a few hours at least, disown myself.

We stayed late in the bar that night and went back to her mother's. We had sex again, this time sneaking into her bedroom. It was more industrial than before. I sensed that she hated me a little for already having a girlfriend and her being second best. And I hated her a little for knowing this of me and still going through with it. So the intimacy was compromised, neither of us truly ourselves. She was silent in the act, shifting from one move to another. I went to talk and she put her finger to my mouth and closed my lips. It was impressive but it felt done for effect as if she'd seen it in a film or perfected it with another lover.

After the first date with Kate I had managed to avoid Sarah for a few days. I told her I had a cold and didn't want her to catch it. I felt slightly less bad because, beyond a cursory inquiry, she didn't ask how I was or turn up with throat pastilles and medicines (I knew this was feeling sorry for myself but we all do it, dreaming that someone cares that much). Finally seeing her again was peculiar. Betrayal makes you feel as if your skin has turned a different colour or there's writing across your forehead: evil, shame, trickster, bastard. Then you notice that they haven't noticed and it's the same as before—wanting you, being with you, loving you, still contacting you at six o'clock every day. But the kindness is painful now. You pity her. While she's holding your hand, looking at you in that way, you know it would take, say, five seconds to end her world. Your world, too. 'I've been with someone else.' The secret dances on your tongue. Time and again you have to swallow it down. I didn't tell Sarah. I was strong. I carried it.

I came home from university most weekends and usually managed to fit in seeing Kate. Sarah often said she was busy on Sunday nights 'getting ready for work' so, over the course of a few weeks, it became routine that I'd see Kate at this time. The evenings followed the same pattern: bar, talk, flirt, back to her place for sex. But the cheating soon started to add up. At first it was okay because I told myself it was an aberration, not really me, we all make mistakes. But I kept making the same mistake. Whenever I left Kate, I'd feel physically sick. I sensed I was being watched. Someone was tallying up all this deceit and logging it down. If the idea was to make myself feel more wanted, more important, more alive, it wasn't working. I was devaluing what I had with Sarah. Taking her from Dan now felt like an act of vainglory that I had no right to dress up as an irresistible compulsion, a once in a lifetime circumstance.

Al was angered by Kizzy's hostile dismissal of the trip idea.

"I don't remember you even being invited," he said.

I told Al I'd ask my dad if I could borrow his van; we could travel in that.

"When do you think this might happen?" he asked.

"As soon as I can get time off uni."

After a few seconds of silence Kizzy asked me:

"Do you remember when you first met us two?"

The question was designed to lead me into a familiar anecdote. The pair had their favourite stories which they liked to hear regularly, much the same as Niall. I had first 'met' them in the early hours of a Sunday morning when I was about thirteen years old; they were a few years older than me. I had heard a commotion and, out of my bedroom window, I recognised Kizzy from seeing him visiting his parents' down the street. They were both drunk and started rolling across a car which I presumed belonged to one of them. They saw me.

"Open your window, kid."

Kizzy started tap dancing on the bonnet.

"How many marks do you give him for artistical impressions?" asked Al.

"Seven."

"Right, I'll beat that."

Al was wearing a thick padded coat. He ran at the car and flopped on it, rolling down and landing on the floor.

"How about that?"

"That's an eight, easily."

He took his right hand in his left and held it aloft as if it were a trophy.

"And the winner, ladies and gentlemen, is Allllllex McDeeeeermott."

He bowed to the houses where lights had started to come on and curtains opened.

The next morning I saw them sitting on the edge of the pavement, rubbing their heads. They said they'd been drinking cider and 'benbos' the previous night.

"What's a benbo?"

"Bitter and lager mixed. Gets you totally out of it—benbo, benbo crazy. A few pints of that stuff and you can't remember your own name."

They had no idea what they'd done the night before. I told them. Every time I went a bit further with the story they looked at one another and said, 'Fucking hell, really?' and burst out laughing.

A few days later, the knackered, bashed-in, danced-on car was towed away—it *had* belonged to them. Soon afterwards they each got motorbikes but these never seemed to work either. They were always lying beneath them, cursing when things wouldn't fit back together. They had me passing them stuff, pulling the brakes while they watched the cable tense and slacken, spraying WD40 on to nuts, scrubbing the engine with a wire brush. Sometimes they cadged tools off my dad. They called him by his first name which made them seem very grown up. Other kids would watch too, asking questions.

"Where's the carburettor?" "Is that the kick-start or the stand?"

Kizzy and Al would tell them to go and play—on the motorway.

"See how many cars you can dodge."

I'd hang about the longest. After a while they'd talk half serious, asking me if I liked school, things like that.

"We never went to school did we, Kizzy?"

"Nah, it's for kids!"

I asked Kizzy why he was called Kizzy.

"My grandad is from Poland and because of him I've got a second name which is unpronounceable, even for me," he joked. "It's got a K at the beginning and a Z somewhere, so, ever since I was knee high to a reet local millworker, I've been Kizzy."

By the time I was seventeen, Kizzy and Al had become two of my best friends.

I dropped them both off at Kizzy's. They lingered around the car, starting up the rigmarole with the roll-up cigarettes all over again. As I set off I had to shoo them clear by shouting through the window.

*

I was expecting to receive a text from Sarah, the routine six o'clock check-in, but there wasn't one. I texted her:

'How you feeling?'

I resolved to give her fifteen minutes to reply and if I didn't hear back I'd text Kate to see if she fancied going out for our routine Sunday night rendezvous. This felt appropriate, leaving it to fate (kind of). Within minutes I heard the phone sound. 'K' appeared on the screen. This was more than fate. The text read: 'Taking me out big boy?' Big boy? I cringed. But, all set then—I'd go out with her. She'd got there first, cared the most. I texted that I'd see her later. Back home, as I washed and shaved, I thought, once more, that I wasn't made for this, too much life with the potential to collide. I'd finish Kate and leave for university in the morning and get out of town, just as they did in films.

Kate looked prettier than ever before, in a black dress with a yellow bead necklace. She'd taken the eyeliner to a point at the corner of her eyes so she looked slightly oriental. She stood close to me at the bar while I ordered. People were staring at her.

"Grab a chair," I said.

When she moved away a middle-aged man sitting on a high stool said:

"You've got a good-looking girlfriend, there."

I nodded. He'd said it sincerely, a thought spoken. I put the drinks on the table.

"It's lovely to see you," she said.

I'd never known her so earnest.

"Thanks, it's nice to see you, too."

"Did you see all those kids queuing up at the cinema?" she asked.

"Yeah, what's that all about?"

"It's the new Harry Potter film, *Harry Potter and the Prisoner of Azkaban.*"

"I hate Harry Potter," I said. "Don't tell me you're a fan."

She nodded and smiled.

It felt like a set-up: her looking so good, the man at the bar, people watching admiringly, her friendliness. I'd planned to finish her swiftly, one drink and out. I changed the plan. I'd see how the night went and make absolutely sure I was doing the right thing. She spoke about herself in more detail than ever before. She said her mother suffered from arthritis and was also an agoraphobic so she had to do most things for her—the shopping, cooking, picking up medication. Her dad had been injured years before when he got caught in a packing machine at work. He survived the accident but died from a heart attack a few months later. The stress of it had got to him, she said. She spoke about him for a while and it was good to see this unassuming, more open side. I wondered whether this was tactical, that she'd sensed I was slipping away and realised giving more was a way to draw me closer.

Her phone sounded; it was a text. I noticed she had a new phone, one that you had to flip open.

"Very *Star Trek*," I said.

I think she thought *Star Trek* was a make of phone.

"No, it's a Motorola RAZR V3, actually. So much more on-point than your poxy Nokia 7610."

"I didn't know you had such a comprehensive knowledge of mobile phones."

"I like my gadgets," she said.

We started talking about our backgrounds, people we knew, schools we'd been to. I realised it was probably unusual that we hadn't talked this way before. I then said something that wasn't even quirky, let alone 'wacky' and she exclaimed:

"You're dead wacky, you, aren't you?"

This single comment turned off the light, slammed the door. There'd been a few things but this was final proof that I was with someone with whom I wasn't meant to be. When someone says you're wacky it grants them a passive role while you become their entertainment for the evening. You feel obliged to become bigger, louder, showing off, though you hate yourself for it because you're not actually being yourself but fulfilling someone else's idea of you. Another irritating habit I'd noticed was her pulling faces in a supposed self-deprecating way. She'd be talking about, say, a work colleague and then add, 'She's really good looking, not like me', before twisting her mouth, wrinkling her nose and going cross-eyed. It was a humility I didn't believe in; she knew she was good-looking.

But I'd left it too late to finish her. Too much smiling and flirting had been going on. I'd do it next time. I drove her home. As we approached her house she asked me to carry on driving.

"How come?"

"I don't want to go back yet."

I parked in a side street.

"I want you to tell me what's wrong," she said.

Christ, she'd noticed. She was slightly drunk, her gaze wavering as if she was looking at me through water.

"Nothing's wrong."

"There is." [She had clearly sensed a detachment.]

"There isn't, honest."

I didn't know how to tell her that a little thing such as calling me wacky had killed us off because I was the kind of ludicrous person who saw portent in everything (well, nearly everything). The face pulling, too. And all those other physiological and personality tics that were becoming more evident every time I saw her: the quizzical raised eyebrow gesture; the too much effort with the make-up; the self-proclaimed love of gadgets; the saying 'Really?' in a loud voice whenever I'd said something pretty ordinary; the overbearing perfume; the fondness of Harry Potter; the cleavage she invariably had on show (now, away from her, when she was the girl planted solely in my thoughts and memory, I liked this because it was sexy and a sign of confidence that she should show off her body, so. But was a girl so happy to reveal that much flesh, to enjoy the flicker and fire between your eyes and the front of her dress—and she did, no doubt about that—genuine girlfriend material?).

Most of all, though, and I felt this intuitively from the beginning, was that you could tell she'd been hurt somewhere along the way and it meant she couldn't relax and be happy in her own skin. Maybe it was her weird sickly mother. Perhaps she had filled Kate's head with oddball stuff, making *her* the parent while she remained a child. Or perhaps Kate's dad had beaten her or another horrible childhood trauma had been inflicted upon her. Or maybe it was the slow-slow disappointment of not being loved enough by her parents or of being loved too much, made to feel too special. It's hard to tell; it's all guesswork. How can you explain that you feel all this about someone and not wreck them forever?

We went back to her house. It wasn't late but her mum was in bed.

"She more or less lives in her room. I have to take meals up to her," said Kate.

"When did she last go out?"

"Years ago. I can't remember seeing her out of her night-clothes to be honest."

While Kate poured herself a glass of wine I looked around the living room. A wedding photograph was on the windowsill. Her dad was easily a foot taller than her mum, dark haired with a moon face, a bit like the henchman in old gangster films.

"Look at your dad's hands," I said.

I was about to blurt: 'No wonder he got them stuck in a bloody machine' but stopped myself in time.

"What do you mean?"

"How big they are."

"Are they?"

He had them by his thigh. They spanned most of the width of his leg. I wondered again if he'd used them on her, whacked her about when she was a kid, turned her into this slightly skew-whiff adult. She got up and took a closer look at the photograph.

"Yeah, you're right I suppose. Can't say I've ever noticed

before. Don't you think he looks kind? He had such nice eyes."

"He was a big bloke, wasn't he?"

"Too right," she said proudly. "Well over six feet."

We had sex on the settee. In all the grunting and sweating her make-up began to smudge like a birthday cake thrown against a window. Afterwards, I closed my eyes.

"Tired?" she asked.

"A bit. I'm going back to uni tomorrow."

"Shall I massage your shoulders for you?"

"I'm okay, thanks."

In the car driving home I fumbled for the phone I'd left in the glove compartment. There were five messages from Sarah:

'Sorry I missed you at 6, fell asleep.'

'Perked up quite a bit. Where U B?'

'Where are U?'

'Answer me do.'

'Worried now. Text me.'

Monday

I left early. If I missed the morning traffic I could do the journey to university in two hours. I got there about fifteen minutes before the first seminar and watched the room filling up. Looking around, I began daydreaming, predicting the type of book everyone was going to write, should they make it to authordom. The quiet ones will do slasher novels—corpses in abandoned garages, blood dripping on to oil and soil, the putrefaction assiduously detailed. They'll throw in some deviant sex, Joe-style, and people the story with drifters (writers are preternaturally obsessed with drifters, I'm not sure why) who find themselves in a motel room or a dense wood or the roof of a building, on the verge of killing themselves or someone else. The odd students such as Barry (his parents must have been spiteful, calling a kid of our generation, Barry) in his zigzaggy black and red cardigan with his bizarre hair parting (formed at the right ear and slung over) will do comic novels. He's already said so. But Big Joe doesn't like comic novels.

"Merely hearing the words 'comic novel' makes me nauseous," he thundered.

Barry said they sold well.

"Yes, but who to?"

"People who like a laugh."

"They're read by people who don't habitually read books. They buy one a year and it happens to be a comic-fucking-novel."

I told Joe I might write books for kids. Niall had given me the idea. We make up stories to keep him entertained because he's spent a lot of time at home, poorly. Whenever I finish, he begs, 'What then, what then?'

"Why choose a framework that sidesteps any consideration of intellectualism and discursive depth?" asked Joe. "Aren't you limiting yourself to the river when you could be swimming out to sea?"

Joe was always like this, straight at you, trying to find out your motives and forever saying, 'How do you mean?' which, when you think about it, you can say to almost anything anyone ever says and force them to keep revealing ever more. I told him kids were more intelligent than he thought.

"But they fall for dumb magic tricks and the myth of Father Christmas."

"Maybe they choose to."

"Good answer but it doesn't mean anything," he said.

In that same session, another student, Melissa, asked about fantasy novels: did Joe put them in a similar category?

"Don't go there," he said.

He went there. These made him sick, too—anything that featured goblins and ghosties or things living in the undergrowth. Eventually someone had to ask.

"What do you like then, Joe?"

Serious face, now.

"Books that shake you up, make you think. Books that tip up your universe and tamper with the consensual status quo. Books that carry great wisdom by virtue of their precision of insight and detail. Books that dip into the pool of shared emotions, the whole gamut of the human condition."

For no obvious reason, he then turned to me.

"What do you like?"

"This and that."

"Come on."

I said the names of a few authors.

"They're all dead," he gasped. "What about contemporary writers?"

I couldn't think who to say.

"Okay then, tell me who you don't like or what you don't like. Let's do it that way round."

"I'm not into things that are absurd, that would never happen in real life."

"What like?"

"You know, magic realism or whatever it's called. Anything with acrobats in it and circuses in general. Stuff like talking dogs. Entities, beings."

He brought his lips together tight and waved his finger as if shaking drops of watery paint from a brush.

"Right, you've told us what you don't like, why don't you now tell us what you do?"

"I like books that ramble on, that are like someone talking to you or you're hearing thoughts. When I meet someone or just see them around I always think: what are you like? What's happened to you? What do you think about and what words do you use to describe things? What would you choose to tell me—you know, what matters to you?"

The room had fallen quiet. The silence was broken with a long and rasping cry of 'Boooooooring' from Joe before he added:

"Go and read Rousseau, my friend. Or that lousy Scottish poet who spent 200 pages telling us his tedious thoughts as he stared at a dandelion or thistle or whatever it was."

"Hugh MacDiarmid," said Barry.

"What about him?"

"He's the poet who wrote *A Drunk Man Looks at the Thistle*."

"Good for him. When did he write the thing?"

"1926."

"Exactly. No one wants that kind of abstract musing these days, all that pointless reverie. They want drive, verve, energy. The buggers want thrilling out of their rinky-dinky little minds."

Barry entered the lecture theatre and sat next to me. I congratulated him on his joust with Joe the previous week, the battle of the comic novel. He said something that I didn't hear and when I asked him to repeat it he jerked his neck and spat:

"He's a tool."

"Who's a tool?"

"Joe's a tool."

At that instant Joe marched into the room chomping on a sandwich, not caring that bits were dropping to the floor. I thought how much he looked the stereotypical lecturer. He was wearing a baggy check shirt that almost reached his knees beneath a corduroy jacket so tatty it might have spent the last few months being booted around the streets. He began handing out sheets of paper. They contained questions such as: what is your father's job? Do you consider yourself rich or poor? Are your parents still together? Do you believe people are essentially good or bad? We filled in our responses and without saying anything he collected them up. He banged the wad on the table, pleased with himself.

"Here in my mitts, folks, I have every novel you lot are ever going to write or attempt to write. It's all here."

"Good for you," said Barry. "But shouldn't you have carried out this exercise on our first week? What's even the point of it?"

"There sometimes isn't a point, Barry. Some things are just

good to do. You know, for fun."

Joe was the last person you'd imagine having 'fun' or doing something without a motive.

He moved on to the main theme of the lecture—the working-class novel. He covered the usual ground: books featuring burly blokes in donkey jackets from Nottingham or Bradford working in factories; bickering boring Sundays in bed-sits; burly blokes in donkey jackets 'seeing' girls called Barbara, Rita, Liz or Doreen (women who were in their teens but looked and acted middle-aged, one of whom would fall pregnant). Joe said these novels dealt with thwarted aspiration, and personally, honestly, if anyone asked his opinion, if he was petitioned to serve up his actual feelings, like, he preferred contemporary books about the working-class because they were not 'hide bound by conventionalism' or the need to tell a 'linear story'.

"Then there's none of that suffocating adherence to a concept of hope and hegira," he said.

Someone asked what hegira meant. He loved being asked the meaning of words or to explain a phrase he'd used. He looked as if he might levitate.

"Exodus, moving on from somewhere. One place to another, a better place. It's from when Muhammad took flight from Mecca to Medina in six hundred and something AD."

Joe asked if anyone had any thoughts. Barry did:

"These books out today, the ones I think you mean. Irvine Welsh and that lot. They're not the same genre at all. They're voyeuristic, postcards from the underclass written by the middle-class. They tell us nothing except the bleakness and hopelessness."

"What about the humour?" said Joe.

"The humour passes itself off as black but it's merely crude. There's no ladder up from the misery. It's circular, perpetual."

Joe said it wasn't a book's duty to falsify hope merely to appease the reader.

"A book without hope," said Barry. "Would attract the reader it deserved: a cynic, a voyeur, someone from a better, safer life, looking down."

Barry might have been eccentric but he was clever.

"Does the unadorned truth offend you, Barry?" asked Joe.

"Not at all. Truth is a subjective determination. You have yours, I have mine. These novels about drugs and violence and stuff, they've been written because they proffer a version of the truth that sells. In other words, a popular truth and nothing more. On the wider issue, what's wrong with telling a story anyway? Surely any writing, the act of putting something down and sharing it, involves a degree of stratagem. You might as well do it with the notion of giving someone pleasure. It's not supposed to be a sufferance."

"There", cried Joe. "That's the difference between us. I think the writer should please himself first and if it makes his reader happy, that's a bonus. Otherwise it becomes a feat of engineering or a commercial exercise rather than artistry or invention. What's that famous John Steinbeck quote? He said a good book should 'rip the reader's nerves to rags'. I'm with him there."

Barry returned to his original query:

"Why have you made us fill in those forms?"

"I'm interested in you lot, what you're about, what class you belong to or what class you *think* you belong to. There's a difference, you know."

An hour had passed in what seemed minutes. This was why I had come to university. I was so absorbed, I'd lost track of who I was, where I was up to in my life: Sarah, Kate, Jenny, Niall, Loachy, Kizzy, Al, all of it.

Afterwards, on the way to the refectory, I saw I had a voice message on my phone. I held it to my ear.

"It's Sarah, can you call me as soon as possible?"

I had texted her the night before, replying to the ones she'd sent while I was with Kate. I guessed she was feeling better and wanted to know if I would be returning home at some point in the week. I slung my bag against the wall on the corridor and phoned her number. It had barely sounded when she answered:

"It's my dad," she said. "He went to the doctor's this morning feeling a bit rough and they've taken him straight to hospital. Mum's with him now and I'm leaving work to go and see him."

"What do they think is wrong?"

"Something to do with his heart but they're not sure."

I'd heard before of people rushed to hospital from the doctor's and it had turned out to be a relatively trivial matter. I told her this and began issuing platitudes, that he'd be okay, he was in the best place, she shouldn't worry.

"I'm bound to worry," she snapped. "My mum says he's wired up to God-knows-what and is struggling to breathe."

I asked her to phone me after she'd seen him.

I had a lecture in the afternoon but skipped it and headed to my accommodation. I was almost there when the phone rang. It was Jenny. She sounded as if she'd been crying. I knew immediately that it was about Niall.

"The hospital has just rung. They've found something wrong with his blood. He's got to have more tests."

"Why?"

"They keep fobbing me off, saying it's some sort of inconsistency."

"They'll probably find he's lacking zinc or iron or something and put him on tablets," I said.

"I think it's more serious than that."

"How come?"

"I just do."

I told her what had happened to Sarah's dad. She would normally have asked lots of questions and told me to pass on her love but she was too preoccupied.

"It's a mother's instinct," she said. "Something's wrong."

I wanted company, to be among people, even if it wasn't to discuss the matter, or matters, at hand. After the first year in halls of residence, I had moved into a shared house. But it wasn't the conventional student arrangement; far from it. I had been late sorting out accommodation and the place was the last on the list given out by residential services. The 'house' was two maisonettes on a council estate, knocked into a single dwelling. The owners, a middle-aged couple called John and Joan, lived on site in what they called the 'east wing'. This comprised of a bedroom and bathroom only, so, most of the time, at least one of them was in the communal lounge. As my dad pointed out, it was very much like living in 'digs' as he'd done when first working away from home in the building trade.

On the day I had signed the tenancy agreement, John and Joan told me they smoked two or three 'ciggies' a day but it was more like two or three dozen. Ashtrays overflowed and packets were left all over the place, jammed down the settee, up Joan's sleeve. She was overweight and wore what she called 'tent dresses' which were cotton and usually floral patterned. John had been unemployed for years and was coat hanger skinny with a long face and bedspring eyebrows. I never saw him in anything but a vest and washed-out tracksuit bottoms which I think he slept in. They had a small mangy dog called Princess (what else?). The television was left on most of the day and when someone came on who John didn't like, invariably a Conservative politician, he'd move to the edge of his chair, yelling abuse. On my first evening there, I remember an advert coming on for Bratz dolls.

"What the hell are they?" he cried. "Horrible bloody things. Is that what kids want to play with these days?"

Joan smiled sweetly.

*

I decided not to tell them about Sarah's dad or Niall.

"You're early," said Joan at the door. "Good job I've nearly got the tea ready."

She showed me to my seat in the kitchen as if I was entering a very intimate restaurant.

"I've done your favourite, lasagne."

She had offered to cook for me soon after I moved in and, not wanting to cause offence, I'd accepted. They treated me well, as if I was a surrogate son. Their real son only came round at Christmas. He'd been a bus driver and crashed one after a lunchtime drinking session. They'd fallen out after John told him he'd been 'bloody stupid'. They didn't seem to have any other family or friends; no one ever visited.

"Tell your pals about us," Joan would say. "There's room for more, you know. One or two, anyway. We might be last on the list because we're a few miles from the university but we shouldn't get overlooked."

She believed the geography was against them, not that they lived on a rough estate or were a bit odd or that students no longer wished to live with middle-aged people they didn't know, as if it was the 1980s; I went home every weekend, so it wasn't so bad for me.

Joan reminded me of my mum or gran except you always felt there was some badness waiting to go off—and it did, soon enough—with her or John because you weren't their real son and taking in students, having to share their personal space, had been forced upon them because benefits didn't provide enough income. Joan often spoke of better times.

"You should have seen John when he'd leave for work in a

71

morning, singing to himself, proud as punch," she said.

Her eyes became watery and I told her not to get upset.

"Thanks love," she said. "You do something with your life. But listen on—never trust anyone."

The only other student staying was Andrew, a doctor's son on a business studies course. Similar to me, he had joined his course late after the other houses had been allocated. He had the bedsit attic room, the biggest in the house. You could tell John and Joan were proud to know him, proud he was living with them. Not many people they knew mixed with sons of GPs.

When I'd not heard from Sarah by 8pm I decided to ring. The call was answered but for a second I couldn't hear anyone speaking. Instead, there was loud sobbing and the sound of the phone being passed through hands. I heard my name mentioned. The phone was finally put to someone's ear.

"Hello love, it's Ann [Sarah's mum]. I'm afraid we've had some bad news—Ian's passed away."

"When?"

"About half an hour ago. He had a heart attack here at the hospital."

"I'm really sorry," I said. "Can I speak to Sarah?"

I heard her mother ask if she was okay to speak.

"Hello," said Sarah. "My dad's died."

"Your mum has just told me."

"He had a massive heart attack. Can you come home?"

"I'll throw a few things in a bag and get there as soon as I can."

I went downstairs to tell John and Joan what had happened.

John was in the lounge watching telly with Andrew. This was extremely unusual; Andrew was seldom in during the evening and, if he was, tended to stay in his room. He was sitting in an armchair, his long legs stretched across the carpet. I sat down and before I could speak Andrew started telling me about the weekend he'd spent with his girlfriend, Emma. It was as if he was diverting the focus from John and himself, disarming some tension. I'd never actually met Emma but he'd told me often that she was ever so cute and clever, beautiful and brilliant. I was about to speak finally, to tell them about Sarah's dad, when I noticed John shifting uncomfortably in his chair.

"That actress, what's her name?" he began. "You know, blonde hair. She was in that programme, the one on last night or it might have been the night before."

Joan entered the room, puffing on a newly-lit cigarette. John said a name, the wrong name. Andrew snorted:

"It wasn't her! Look, John, get that prehistoric brain in gear, will you?"

He was smirking and didn't notice John glaring at him. Some badness was about to go off. Now, of all times.

"I'm not having this in my own house," boomed John. "Being spoken down to by a little shit like you. [Andrew was at least six feet, four inches.] You can pack your bloody bags, you can."

"You're joking. This is a joke, right?"

"I'm not bloody joking, no."

"Where's he going to go, John?" I asked.

"That's not my problem, is it? He should have thought about that before he tried to make a fool of me…"

It looked as if he was going to cry but a second later, he spat:

"…in front of my own fucking wife."

When Andrew went upstairs to pack I told them I was going, too. At first they thought it was a show of solidarity.

"You've done nowt wrong, lad," said John. "It's that cocky bleeder what's caused all the upset. He's had it coming."

I explained what had happened to Sarah's dad and they fell solemn instantly, telling me to hurry back home. Before leaving, I asked Andrew to text me later and let me know whether he'd found somewhere to stay.

"Will do, PS," he said. This was his nickname for me, 'Pretend Student'. I was a PS, he claimed, for several reasons—I didn't smoke dope or drink excessively; I was 'ridiculously old' because I'd taken a few years out before going to university; I spent every weekend back home and, finally, creative writing wasn't a proper degree subject because, 'anyone could do it'.

On the drive home I realised the mess I was in. During times of crisis, life crash-bang impacting like this, you were supposed to know your feelings. I felt unclean, having this other girl to think about (Kate) when my bona fide girlfriend (Sarah) was going through so much. I resolved to finish Kate when all this was over; you needed life simple and straightforward when people were dying.

I stopped for a coffee at a motorway service station and tapped out a text to Kate: 'Sarah's dad has died. I'll be in touch later.' She replied within a couple of minutes. I was taken aback by the sensitivity of her message: 'Be strong. I'll be thinking of you. X'

As I turned off the motorway junction nearest home, Andrew phoned.

"PS, is that you? Great news, I'm sorted!" he chirped. "Really sorted."

I asked what he meant.

"I've been offered a room in a house, sharing with two girls. And they're both hotties."

"What about Emma?"

"Who's Emma?" he laughed.

I wasn't sure whether I envied him or not. I knew John and Joan's was a disaster but it formed perfect material for a budding writer. And wasn't there something heroic about trying to sleep in a box room above the lounge, the telly blaring out, hearing them coughing and spluttering and sniping at one another, and Princess yapping away night after night while the hoodies threw cans at one another on the street outside? Surely that was better for shaping the soul than an easy threesome in a candle scented semi-detached on a tree-lined street across the posh side of town. Surely.

Friday, a week later

I took the week off from university. Sarah was incredibly strong as she phoned numerous people informing them of her dad's death. She was faced constantly with petty bureaucracy that must have cut her up but the only indicator of distress was when her fingers clenched occasionally into a fist. She sometimes wept in the evenings but they were quiet, dignified tears.

On the day of the funeral the weather was fitting: damp, grey and gluey. I parked up near Sarah's house. A throng of neighbours huddled outside the front door. As I approached I heard them say:

"Who's he?"

"Sarah's boyfriend."

The coffin was in the front room with the lid off. No one had warned me about this but people milled around as if it was perfectly normal; it might have been the tradition at their particular church. I didn't look directly inside but was aware of the colour yellow. Faces turned to me. I didn't recognise most of them. I nodded, all the same. I pushed open the kitchen door. Before I'd properly entered, her mother put her arms around me. She felt small and round, her dress smooth. Sarah was beyond her, waiting her turn. She buried her head in my shoulder. As we pulled apart, I saw that the crying had picked out her eyes giving them an inky shine and her funeral clothes, silky and dark, fell upon her handsomely. She was saying my name and gripping me tightly. A plate was thrust towards me.

"Would you like a piece of pie?"

"No, thanks."

Ann asked if I'd like to, 'take a look at Ian'.

"It'll help you with the grieving, seeing him at peace."

A chair was by the coffin. I sat on it. The corpse was covered by a yellow silk sheet. The face and hands were the only exposed parts as if it was floating on a lake with only these bits breaking the surface. It was difficult to map out the rest of his body, where his feet ended, the whereabouts of his waist, his chest. Nothing had prepared me for this. I thought

I was familiar with death from films and books but this was different. The flesh was a colour I'd never seen before—white, light red, light yellow, light blue, all mixed up. His head was flat like a discarded mask and he was determinedly dead not only in his skin but also the lips, the eyelids, the knuckles, everything. I moved away and Ann leaned over and held Ian's hand for a few seconds. She then kissed him tenderly on the lips before the two men from the funeral directors put the lid on.

We left the house, climbed into the big black cars and set off. The traffic clogged up behind us. I liked this: a person's last stand against the world, a final jolt of power and influence. Some of those out walking didn't notice us pass by; too busy being alive. Others stopped. Old people, especially. A few made crosses on themselves. An old man halted, took off his hat and saluted. He didn't move until the last car in the procession went by. I swallowed hard.

At the cemetery I watched Sarah's calves stretch tight as she got out of the car. I felt bad for fancying her at such an inappropriate time. Then I thought it was perhaps a good thing—Ian might have died but he'd left behind something special. I had an imaginary conversation with him. He'd become more lyrical and progressive after death. He said it was okay, he knew young men were plagued by carnal desires but he saw also that I loved her for her soul, the light that shone within. I suddenly had a disturbing thought. Now he was omnipresent and telepathic: did he know about Kate?

In the chapel the vicar said we had come together as one to pay tribute to the dearly departed Ian Gould, a cheerful, considerate man. I looked about me, wondering how everyone was keeping a straight face. Ian was the original industrial-issue grouch. Their front room had been a theatre for a long-running one-man play that made Beckett seem a song and dance man. He'd stride in, washed-out shirt hanging down to his trousers, face like a flitting. Everyone was against him, he mewled, ganging up on him, the world and its wife on his back again. He swore a lot for a church goer, too.

"What's this on telly?" he'd start. "What do you want this on for? It's boring, is this. Doesn't make any sense, all this jumping around, acting the goat. What's it supposed to be, a comedy? Because it's not funny, not funny at all. And where's the paper? Someone's bloody had it. I left some forms from work over there too, on the sideboard. Same every time in this house. Always some bugger moving something. Is it like this where you live?"

He often dragged me into arguments, looking for an ally. But going to his side meant deserting the other—Sarah and her mum. I could only sideways smile, trying to show I was stuck in the middle.

"Say what you're thinking, don't be shy."

Most of the time it had all been good fun but you could never tell with Ian. Once or twice he was nasty to Ann, calling her bloody stupid and telling her she didn't have the brains she was born with. Usually, when he'd had enough, he flounced into the kitchen and we'd hear cupboard doors slamming. His revenge on the world seemed to be clumsily warming up soup from a tin or going upstairs to bed with cake and tea, banging down hard with every footstep.

After the service we moved on to the graveside. While

we were standing there, a huddle of women behind me were talking and looking down. I turned around and they pointed to a tiny frog in the grass.

"Pick it up, will you? It might get trodden on."

I reached down, scooped it up and put it on the other side of a gravestone.

The vicar was close to the open grave, reading aloud from the Bible. He was tall, probably in his late forties, with a thin moustache and long nose. He wore glasses and, with his hands occupied clutching the Bible, he tried to move them higher up his face by twitching his eyebrows and the top of his cheeks. He spoke in a singsong northern accent. When he finished, people took handfuls of dry earth and threw it on to the coffin. Sarah wasn't sure of the protocol and whispered:

"Do we have to throw some as well?"

I shrugged my shoulders. She picked some up anyway and sprinkled it down the hole. I couldn't see the coffin but heard the earth pitter-patter on the wood. As the party dispersed, I stared down at the coffin. The hole was deeper than I had expected. He wasn't buried a few feet under, in soft spongy soil and still within tapping distance of the living world. He was right down there among lumpy grey matter that carried no life, not even worms or beetles. The other funerals I'd been to had been cremations and I'd imagined that when the bodies were burned they billowed from the fire and scattered like grey leaves from a brazier. They were still, partially at least, above the earth and subject to light and dark, the sun and the rain. It seemed callous leaving Ian alone, locked so far down into the dark like that, as though we were going against nature.

We moved on to a pub for the wake. The vicar toured the room and asked everyone how they knew Ian. He carried a pint of beer and took small but bold sips. The old ladies teased him that he shouldn't be drinking on duty and he relished the attention. I'm not sure I liked his chumminess.

I asked Sarah if she minded if I went out later with Kizzy and Al; they usually had a bender on Friday nights. She looked perplexed for a moment but then smiled.

"You might as well. I'll just be at home with mum making ham sandwiches for any lingering relatives," she said. "And you've had a long week with all this and the worry about Niall."

I was touched by her level of consideration.

When I got to Kizzy's it seemed as if every light in the house was switched on. Music was blaring out. Kizzy answered the door, Al a few feet behind. The smell of aftershave was overwhelming.

"How did it go at Smiler's passing out parade?" asked Kizzy.

After the solemnity of the rest of the day, this irreverence was sweet relief.

"Not bad. It was a good job the lap dancers turned up, that's all I can say."

Al chucked me a can of beer.

"Guzzle on that pup."

We got a taxi into town. The beer was necked down, benbo style. They were both on the lookout for girls. They'd been on the lookout for years without much success. All the things you were supposed to do—glancing over, chancing a smile, brushing past, talking to them—it seemed a foreign language to them. I wasn't much better but was at least aware of the etiquette, that it involved not being your normal true shy self for a few minutes until a connection was made. Kizzy seldom approached anyone but at least Al tried, even if it was to talk about subjects he covered when he was out walking the moors with us, which probably wasn't the stuff girls really wanted to hear about. He'd inform them that there was once a Roman settlement within two miles of where they were now standing and tools discovered nearby could be carbon-dated to the Neolithic period. They really wanted small talk, of course, at least to start with: 'Where do you work?' 'Do you like your job?' 'Can I buy you a drink?' When Al spoke you could see it baffled them. The zeal probably unsettled them, too. You weren't supposed to get that excited about digging up rusty bits of metal.

We moved on to a nightclub. The DJ appeared to play the same two tracks continually—Peter Andre's *Mysterious Girl* and *Toxic* by Britney Spears. Everyone was dancing and whooping, completely oblivious to the cheesiness of the music. The three of us could each sense the night slipping away, becoming ordinary. I was happy merely to be drunk but they remained determined to wring more from the night; men on a mission. Al chatted with a few girls but they were clearly uninterested, looking beyond him, not making eye contact. He had a bottle of vodka in his trouser pocket and was becoming increasingly conspicuous as he took ever more gulps.

"Let's get back," I said.

"Might as well. It's shit here," said Al.

Back at Kizzy's they poured themselves excessive helpings of neat vodka. Al started complaining about the girls 'around here'. Full of themselves, they were. Who did they think they were? Kizzy joined in but with a more embittered tone.

"They're all rough, basically."

Al pointed at me:

"You, you're all right. You've got Sarah and all those girls at university. They're fit, they are, I bet. That's what we need, some girls like that, college girls. They're all chavs, here. Honest to God, they are. I don't think there's one girl who wears corduroy skirts."

"What?" shrieked Kizzy.

"Posh girls, smart girls, they wear corduroy skirts. I've noticed. And they have long hair and wash it more, they do. And comb it so it looks nice down their back. So you want to stroke it."

Al was tired, head falling to his chest. His words were on ice, sliding together:

"Theydontwashtheirhairenoughthegirlsaroundhere."

Kizzy pierced Al's fog:

"It's your own fault."

"What's my own fault?"

Fully cognisant now, Al turned to face Kizzy in the exaggerated way of a drunk, stopping the movement abruptly as if his head might otherwise go all the way round.

"What you talking about?" asked Al.

"You, you'll never pick anyone up the way you go about it."

"I fucking will."

"You fucking won't."

"Why not?"

"You talk crap."

I tried to make the peace.

"Come on, cool it."

The taxi I had ordered drew up outside. I stood in the middle of the room and held out my hands like a referee separating two boxers, except these two were already knocked out, slumped on either side of the room.

"Let's leave it now," I said.

They nodded and it looked as if they were about to fall asleep.

Saturday

The next morning I called back round at Kizzy's to see how they were. The front door was unlocked.

"Hello, anyone in?"

I could hear snoring. One body was in a chair, the other on the floor pressed close to the fire. A coat was over one, a threadbare sleeping bag, the other. The smell of last night's aftershave had been superseded by fags and beer. They hadn't 'left it' when I'd gone home. They'd gone bloody mad. The coffee table was in splinters. Shards of glass were over the carpet. Patches of blood dabbed the walls. Al came round first, coughing, drawing phlegm up from his chest, desperate for the first fag of the day. He had a black eye.

"What happened?" I asked.

"It kicked off a bit last night after you'd gone."

"A bit? The house is wrecked."

"We knocked a few things over. It'll soon straighten up. I shouldn't have let him get to me like that. I usually fire off home when he starts."

Kizzy woke up and the pair were surprisingly cordial to one another considering the fury of a few hours earlier.

"Do you want a brew, Cunty?" Kizzy asked Al.

After we'd drunk the tea, I gave Al a lift home. He was quiet, staring ahead.

"It shouldn't get to that, knocking fuck out of each other," he said, eventually. "It's the frustration, see. Living around here and having shit jobs. It gets to you. I know you've got stuff on with Sarah's dad dying and Niall being ill and all that but at least you've got university and a decent career to look forward to."

He fell silent again but then added:

"We've got to get away. We need a break."

I liked that both Al and Kizzy genuinely believed that a short holiday or even something as basic as a change in the weather, a good meal or a cup of strong tea could lead to better things.

Monday

Niall was due to attend the hospital for more tests so I decided to stay at home a day longer; I wanted to be around whatever the news. When they got back, Jenny said they had treated him 'like a pin cushion', injecting him to see if he was allergic to different things; drawing blood up into phials and slotting them into small wooden racks; X-raying him; putting pads on his chest; wiring him up to a machine and making him breathe into tubes.

"We'll have the results in a week or so," she said.

"How are you coping?" I asked.

"I'm not sure I am."

Tuesday

I was glad to be back at university. Back to normal. As we filed out of the lecture theatre at lunch time, Joe tapped me on the shoulder.

"Can I have a word?"

"Sure."

He asked me to sit down and he did the same across the narrow aisle. He stretched out his legs. His thighs looked huge wrapped tight in black denim. His shoes were scuffed, dried muck up the sides. He wanted to know where I was going, you know, with my writing, what I hoped to achieve. He said I 'interested him'. I shrugged. He threw me a book.

"She's written her life, more or less, then dressed it up as a piece of fiction. Have you heard of her?"

"No."

A blurry photograph of trees was on the cover, the routine signal that this was a book of modern (cutting edge) literature—the cover of Simon's book of poetry had been very similar. On the inside, nearly as big as life, was a photo of the author's face. She was a young, peachy skinned girl with pouty lips.

"Is it any good?" I asked.

"Not bad. It covers your kind of subject matter but has the level of restraint I'm trying to put across to you lot. It's just cool, somehow."

I didn't like it straight away: the cover, the photo, the first sentence.

"I'm not going to read it," I said.

"How come?"

I was feeling unusually confident.

"Life's too short. I don't want to spend time with someone I don't want to be with."

"I can understand that but how do you know before you've even read it or at least scanned it?"

"This photo here. They've suckered her, haven't they, because she's young and pretty. I bet they tell us her age somewhere, hang on…"

It did, she was twenty three.

"See. It's a marketing exercise."

He tutted.

"Ouch, hark the cynic," he said. "I thought that was my job! It might be that her editor is playing the game, using anything he or she can to get the book moving, get it across to people. So, they've flagged it up as this new kid on the block. If it works, gets people interested, it's worth it, isn't it?"

I asked him to spare me a few minutes while I read the opening pages. He began checking his phone for messages. I made quick headway; the type was practically double-spaced.

"The writing is too cool." I said. "It's risk free. She writes bloodlessly. You know, where everything has this thinness of expression which is mistaken as a signifier of integrity or gravity. There's nothing here, nothing to care about."

"It's had good reviews."

"It will do. It still doesn't matter, it won't connect with people."

"Her last one sold quite well."

"That's a shame."

I sensed I was annoying him.

"Anyhows [this was one of his turns of phrase designed to move progress], that's not the main reason I wanted a chat today."

A door opened behind us. It was the cleaner everyone called Swoop. He had the misfortune of having a beaky nose, so looked bird-like as he swooped down to pick up discarded toffee wrappers or leaflets.

"Come on, what are you two ladies jabbering about?" he said. "There's a bloke here that needs to get his work done. Can't be hanging around all day."

"Looks like we'll have to reconvene at a later date," said Joe.

Friday

Jenny rang and said she'd been asked to attend the hospital on Friday afternoon. I said I'd go with her.

"Mum's coming," she said.

"What about dad?"

"You know how he is. He's best staying at home, getting Niall to and from school."

Dad hated hospitals, doctors, dentists, surgeries, white coats. He believed that once the medical profession got at you with its pills, probes, scalpels and half-baked ideas, you were doomed. Mum and Jenny made a big deal of this, how silly he was, but I understood his stance. You had to love life an awful lot to feel the way he did about possibly losing it.

I travelled back on Thursday evening and arranged to see Loachy the next morning before the hospital appointment. I was going to ask him to join me and Al on our grand tour of England—we'd planned it over several e-mails through the week.

We met at the Copa Café in town. The woman who owned it had gone for a minimalist approach to decor by simply painting everything black, even the floor and tables. It had been done about a year earlier but still smelled faintly of paint. Loachy was there when I arrived, running his finger around the rim of his coffee cup and dabbing froth on his tongue. He started talking about work, how they were cutting investment. Redundancies had been mooted, especially in the art department which, he said, had always been a low priority.

"I'll never get that," he said. "Life *is* art. All the other subjects are supplementary rather than elemental."

As he spoke, someone dressed as Superman walked in the café. Loachy's discourse on college politics had run for several minutes and I guessed this was big enough news to cut him short.

"There's Superman," I said.

I realised it was a girl, not a man. Maybe it was Supergirl or Superwoman, I thought. No, they had different costumes. She shuffled over to our table. She was collecting for charity. She looked forlorn.

"Hello, I wondered if you'd like to…"

She'd hardly got started when Loachy told her:

"We like to support charities in our own way, with private donations."

The abruptness of Loachy's response made her blush. She was only a kid, just out of school. She moved on to the next table. I'd have given her something, not caring whether it went to charity or her own pocket or to a dubious organisation that only gave one per cent to handicapped children or abandoned donkeys. It took great courage and commitment to walk around dressed as Superman in bulky shoulder pads and a red cape, constantly repositioning the kiss curl on your forehead.

I started to think about Loachy, speaking for us both like that. And how he was totally, brazenly unapologetic about being *an artist*. He didn't shilly-shally or fret. He knew his rightful rarefied place, his standing in the world. I wanted to be like that, like him. Sure of myself as a writer. What made him like he was and me like me? My mum and dad had believed that the cardinal requirement of good parenting was to make sure their kids never got too big for their boots. So if you spoke for too long, you were asked if you liked the sound of your own voice. Or if you showed signs of enjoying your intelligence, you were a 'clever arse'. And should you show a bent for singing, painting, joking or performing, this was okay, so long as you didn't get too full of yourself, kid. While this was going on, what was happening on the other side of town, at Loachy's house? Was he told to carry on talking, carry on singing? Were his childhood paintings filling every inch of space on the walls? Or maybe his upbringing had been the same as mine but he'd nurtured a greater defiance and *made* them listen to him. Am I remembering it accurately, anyway? Do we each want to believe we were hard done to? Doesn't everyone hold out their childhood as a warty toad on the palm of their hand? If my parents did go easy on the praise (and they might not have done, it's all relative), had it not made me pragmatic, given me a true sense of value? Sometimes, when Loachy talks, his eyes ablaze, gushing about his art so expressively, I *don't* want to be like him. It's never phoney—he always means it—but after a while you realise that self-doubt and vulnerability are, in fact, necessary qualities in a person and their absence soon becomes noticeable, regrettable even.

We finally got round to discussing the trip.

"Who else is coming?" asked Loachy.

"Al," I said.

"Al?"

"Yeah, Al."

He grinned and held my gaze for a few seconds.

"He'll be after girls all the time," he said.

"You can talk!"

"It's different with me, you know it is. Don't you think me and him will make for rather incompatible fellow travellers?"

"Not really. It's all part of the fun, anyway. As long as you don't start patronising or lecturing him, we'll be fine."

"All right," he said. "I'll put it down to experience."

Once the funeral and all the bureaucracy was over, Sarah, like someone who had held their breath for an inordinate amount of time, breathed out her anguish and pain in torrents. She sobbed so hard that she was sometimes unable to stand up, putting her hands against furniture or the walls to stay balanced. When she rallied, she spoke for hour after hour about her dad; it seemed there wasn't a single incident from her childhood involving him that she didn't mention. She painted Ian as this heroic, dignified figure and I struggled to relate it to the likeable but grumpy bloke who had roamed their house. I should have known him when he was younger, she said, when he was cheerful and full of life. She eulogised their relationship, suggesting they had an especially close father-daughter bond, though I recalled them arguing regularly with lots of yelling and arms often thrown in the air in exasperation. I supposed this was typical family life, good and bad frothing up but always love beneath it all.

On the drive to the hospital mum spoke incessantly. She was troubled by what Jenny had been told over the phone before Niall had gone in for tests. She hated ambiguity.

"Something wrong with his blood—what's that supposed to mean?"

We had to wait nearly an hour in the reception area. Mum was growing impatient, asking whether they'd forgotten about us, had the girl on the desk keyed into her computer that we'd arrived? Niall's name finally lit up fluorescent red on the screen. Mum and me trailed Jenny down the corridor. The consultant held open the door and when I passed he looked around as if expecting more to follow on, making a joke about the size of our party. Jenny sat across from him at his desk while we flanked her on either side, standing.

"I'm afraid Niall has a blood disorder but what exactly it is we can't quite determine at this moment in time," he said. "Whatever it is, we've discovered it extremely early."

Jenny blurted: "Is it cancer?"

The consultant said he couldn't rule out that they might have found evidence of leukaemia, though the tests were inconclusive.

"What chance has he got? What chance has he got to live?" she repeated.

"Please try not to be alarmed. We need to do more tests. Monitor the situation. Find out why the white blood cells are behaving abnormally."

"Abnormally?"

She was scavenging on his every word. He suddenly came over all colloquial, making it sound like a rogue line dancing team:

"They're doing one thing when they should be doing another."

Mum put her hand on Jenny's shoulder. He saw the movement.

"I fully understand how worried you might be but please

try and remain positive."

Mum asked if he had kids himself. He smiled.

"Two boys. One is at university and the other still at home."

"You'll know how we're feeling then."

He nodded and then did something that made mum fill up with tears whenever she mentioned it later. He stopped jabbing at the computer keyboard and looked at us straight on. He was Indian and spoke in a clipped English accent.

"We'll do our level best for the boy."

Mum said we had his word now. And he had such a kind face—'lovely brown eyes', which she mentioned repeatedly. Jenny missed the moment. She'd stopped listening. Worry had spirited her away from the room.

Afterwards we went to a café in the town centre, the one in the shopping precinct where pensioners could have 'toasties' and a slice of cake for a set price. A piano was at the entrance. While we waited for our food, the old-boy pianist turned up. He had white hair and polished black shoes. He nodded, issued a slick professional smile as he lifted the piano lid and leaned into the microphone.

"Good afternoon, ladies and gentlemen."

He began: "I see trees of green, red roses too…"

Mum and Jenny nibbled on dry sandwiches. Mum said she was 'sick to her stomach' with worry about Niall. Jenny appeared to be in a trance, her eyes red and watery, answering questions with either a yes, no or shrug. They left most of their food. I wanted to be alone, to move to the next scene as if, by doing so, it would help me get used to the idea of Niall being seriously ill or at least allow me to escape the suffocation of our communal grief.

They said they had some shopping to do and would catch the bus home or get a taxi. I left them and ambled through the precinct towards the car park. Suddenly, I saw, walking towards me, about twenty metres away, Sarah. With another man. I had only a second to process the scene, enough time to endure a booming heartbeat that almost caused me to faint. They did not look as if they were lovers (my first thought, obviously). There was nothing furtive about them, how they moved in relation to one another, where their eyes were set. In fact, their togetherness appeared almost humdrum, as if they had been given jobs to carry out and were doing them in parallel. He was of medium build and dark-haired. Already, in that granule of time, I had done that thing all men do of other men: weighed him up, balanced him against me. I played it cool.

"Hello," I said.

"Hello," replied Sarah, big-eyed and blinking.

She was nervous but I sensed immediately it was because of how the situation looked, not how it was necessarily. She pointed to the man at her side.

"This is Ben," she said. "We're going for a coffee to run through this week's workload."

"Hello, Ben," I said, looking into his eyes, testing his nerve. I offered him my hand to shake. He took it.

"All right, mate," he said.

Sarah asked if I wanted to join them. Then, as if she had reeled through her thoughts and fixed the appropriate one in the frame, gasped:

"How did you get on at the hospital?"

"Not bad, I'll tell you about it when I see you tonight."

"Everything was okay though, wasn't it?"

"Yeah."

I said I didn't have time for a coffee. I wanted to come across as the type of bloke who was so self-assured that he didn't mind his girlfriend hanging out with another man in a public place. Women liked that level of confidence and trust. As I walked off I wondered if, however, it might be misconstrued as indifference, stupidity even. Women also liked to feel wanted, to know their partner held a degree of possessiveness and was at least a little uneasy about them spending time with other men.

On the drive home I imagined Sarah leaving me, the devastation. I was mashed up that she was sitting, talking, possibly laughing with another man. I struggled to recall her smiling since her dad's death and thought of all the hours spent talking about him, the crying, and the feeling that we were both draped in darkness, stuck beneath it. She hadn't looked that way as she walked with Ben. She appeared her old self —alive, purposeful, in the moment. But, I told myself, you can't accurately gauge a person's mood or feelings by taking a mental snapshot of them as they walk through a shopping precinct with a work colleague: what was I thinking?

I had to shake the mood, diffuse it. I reached for my phone and texted Kate. She responded saying she had arranged to go out with friends. She sounded disappointed: 'Would have loved to have seen ya too'. Ya? I winced.

Later, I phoned Sarah. She said she was tired and, anyway, her mum was having a bad day so she had best stay at home with her.

"It was nice seeing you today," I said.

She had obviously momentarily forgotten.

"This afternoon, in town. With that Ben bloke," I said.

"Oh, yes. We've been so busy at work, it slipped my mind."

She suddenly remembered:

"Oh God, how did it go with Niall?"

I explained and she said there was a woman at work, Angie, whose grandson used to have leukaemia but had made a full recovery.

"He'll be fine, try not to worry," she said.

I was supposed to be working on an assignment contrasting first person narratives in various American novels, among them books by Mary McCarthy, Raymond Carver and Paul Auster. I was restless in my room and the sound of mum and dad arguing downstairs (probably about Niall) was chipping away at my peace. I decided to visit Al, ostensibly to sort out the trip but mainly for something to do, someone to be with. I'd do the university work later.

He lived in a rented terraced house a mile or so from Jenny's. The place was full of knackered computers, video recorders and games consoles. Next to the busted and sagging settee, piled to knee height, were bits from telescopes, microscopes, theodolites, radios and other contraptions. There was no concession for particular spaces—kitchen, bedrooms, toilet—everywhere was full of junk. The centrepiece in his front room was the 'Beer Can Giraffe', a triangular shaped stack of empty cans that hugged the outline of the fireplace before coming to a point at the ceiling. In his bedroom (which was missing a door) were scattered copies of *The Unexplained* and *Fortean Times* magazines; mounted insects in frames; a collection of matchboxes and beer mats; and various stuffed birds and animals in glass cases. He was the last person in Britain, possibly the world, to still collect video tapes. He had thousands, purchased job-lot at car boot sales or from charity shops. He said he had enough video recorders to last a lifetime and, therefore, could assemble the consummate film library.

"But you won't have any films that were made after they stopped making videos."

"I never thought of that!"

He pointed to a machine on the coffee table.

"That's one of the originals," he said proudly. "A genuine JVC model. If you wandered into Dixons in 1978, that beauty would have set you back nearly £800, roughly £3,000 in today's money. The dreaded digital versatile disc players were launched in 1995 and so the death knell did sound for VHS tapes and players. Did you know Toshiba had originally called them digital *video* discs?"

He was often like this, over-informed on particular, peculiar subjects.

After the obligatory cup of over-sugared tea, he told me Kizzy had reiterated that he wouldn't be joining us on the trip. The issue, it seems, was the van. As a self-professed travel fundamentalist, he considered it poor form to do it on wheels. All you needed, he'd told Al, was a rucksack, sleeping bag, compass, map, a bit of food and a tent. That was it—no worrying about petrol, insurance and where you'd leave your car, all that hassle. The idea was to free up your mind, not get it all blocked up before you started, worrying about this and that, possessions and paraphernalia.

"He's a funny fucker," said Al.

He fished about in the back pocket of his combat trousers and pulled out a grubby piece of paper. It was a list of places he wanted to visit: Housesteads (site of a Roman garrison next to Hadrian's Wall); Fountains Abbey; Stonehenge; Tintern Abbey; Wells Cathedral; Berkeley Castle; Land's End. We were going to work our way down the country, stopping off at these landmarks and also calling at 'show villages' he'd found in an old guide book: Grasmere (Westmorland), Amberley (Sussex), Broadway (Worcestershire), Castle Combe (Wiltshire), Clovelly (Devon), Dunster (Somerset), Finchingfield (Essex), Lower Slaughter (Gloucester), Shere (Surrey) and Boscastle (Cornwall).

"All in one week?" I asked.

"We can give it a go. Nothing to lose."

The evenings were to be set aside for what Al called 'carousing'. Find a pub. Meet the local girls. Raise high the frothing delight.

"We're sure to cop off," he said. "We'll be different than the usual lads they come across. All we have to do is start talking and they'll hear our unfamiliar accents. They're bound to be intrigued."

He offered to print off the list and began tracing wires under and across discarded magazines and scrunched up newspapers on the floor. As the printer finally shunted to life I told him that Loachy would be coming with us. I acknowledged that we made an unlikely trio.

"That's fine," he said. "He can be a patronising twat at times but he means well. He'll come in useful, I suppose, having the gift of the gab. I'll incorporate him into my strategy—he can go in first, do most of the chatting up and I'll clean up after him!"

Al might have filled his house with contraptions and collections, oddments and beer can giraffes, but, more than anything, he was into girls. He coveted the seriously attractive, preferably in a low-cut top, high heels and a short skirt. Sometimes, we'd be out, usually after a few drinks, and he'd identify one clearly outside his league (everyone's league) and begin planning their sexual itinerary.

"I'm going to seduce her in a minute, get her back to mine and show her what's what until she's howling for mercy."

I didn't know whether to mock his conceit and delusion or admire his ambition.

After passing me the printed sheet, he put a hand to his forehead.

"I'm so sorry," he said. "I completely forgot to ask about Niall. You went to the hospital about him today, didn't you?"

I told him the tests had been inconclusive and more were needed. I didn't say that the consultant had mentioned leukaemia. In fact, I had managed to put this out of my head: no point in worrying about something like that until it was confirmed. You heard about lots of kids recovering from leukaemia anyway, these days, like the one Sarah mentioned;

it wasn't necessarily the end. There were a few seconds of silence before he said:

"He's a good kid, Niall."

You didn't have to make speeches or wring out emotion when you were as sincere as Al.

Tuesday

I had another week to do at university before 'spring reading week' which was when we were planning the 'Grand Tour'. After a lecture, Joe asked me to meet him in his study. The appraisals had previously taken place in either the refectory or one of the 'hot spots' dotted around the faculty. I had to ask him the whereabouts of his study. He pointed to an outbuilding swathed in trees.

"That's where they put us to fester, to think until we're completely thunked," he said.

I joined him there an hour or so later. Hundreds of books, possibly thousands, lined one wall in dark wood cases. An angle poise lamp was on the table in the corner, next to a kettle. One or two half-empty bottles of sherry and vodka were dotted around. A print of a harbour scene hung above an old armchair. He saw me looking at it.

"That's Brixham in Devon," he said. "I went there as a kid. The picture used to be at my mother's. I brought it here when she died."

I noticed a dark patch running along the top of the print and stains in one or two places trailing to the boats bobbing on the waves.

"There was a leak in the bathroom and water ran down the wall to the room below. It got under the frame and caused that staining."

I said it was a shame.

"Not really. It reminds me of that day, all of us going round to help mum, trying to find the source of the leak. I remember we were telling her afterwards to throw the picture away but she wasn't having any of it. She said she'd been going to Brixham all her life and couldn't part with it. Me and my brother used to sit and fish on that breakwater, just there, with dad yelling at us that we were doing it all wrong."

He was sitting in the swivel chair at the desk and motioned that I should sit in the armchair. The surface of the desk was barely visible, covered in magazines, tissues, pens, a tatty dictionary and papers waiting to be marked. Another print was above his computer monitor, of three small boats drifting across water in the dark.

"That's the Caves of Drach in Majorca. Have you ever been there?"

I said I hadn't.

"You've got to go. I know people always say that but you really have. It's a huge underground cavern. You go in, this long line of tourists, and they sit you down on wooden benches in what is effectively a natural auditorium. They turn the lights off and you're in absolute darkness, total blackout. Suddenly this music starts up, Albinoni's *Adagio*, and the boats come into view with shadowy people inside carrying candlelit lanterns. It's so peaceful you feel as if your heartbeat is going to get slower and slower until it stops but the funny thing is that you don't mind, it feels right, as if you're dying a happy and perfect death somehow."

I didn't know what to say. I was quite touched. He looked utterly serene. By merely looking at the picture, the blacks, the blues, the oranges, you sensed the tranquillity. He was back there.

"Another thing," he said. "Imagine that while all kinds of things have gone on in the world, empires built and fallen, wars, famines, births, deaths, pain, suffering—that cavern has been there, unchanged for all that time, waiting for someone to illuminate it, to put on a light and show its beauty."

I wondered for a second if all this was an extended metaphor and he was trying to tell me something.

"Anyhows, enough," he snapped. "Do you know how long I've been here, at this college?"

"Ten years?"

"And the rest! Twenty two years. You'd have been a kid when I started here. Twenty two years. A long, long time. You see a lot of changes in twenty two years. And most of the time you just go with it. You know, rolling along. Sometimes I think it's best not to stop and look because when you do you might not like what you see. You might see what you've known was there all along but you've been staring through it and beyond it because you didn't want to see what's directly in front of you. Am I making sense, Boo Boo?"

"I'm not sure."

"No, I'm probably not. But before we're done it's all going to be crystal clear, I promise you. As clear as the fucking lake in the Caves of Drach, where you can see through to all the

102

tiny stones underneath, every detail—so long as you put the light on."

So it was a metaphor! He sat back in the chair. It creaked. I was a little unnerved. I looked about me. He lurched forward.

"Fear not, I'm not going to keep you much longer [it had only been a few minutes]. I know how you kids are today. I suppose you're a gamer like the rest of them, your brain half-nibbled away by all that crash, bang, mutilation."

I told him I didn't play video games.

"Really?"

He moved aside some papers on his desk to find a handwritten note.

"So you won't be wetting yourself in excitement over the prospect of *Grand Theft Auto: San Andreas*, *Halo 2* and *Half-Life 2*—all due later this year I'm informed by one of your contemporaries."

I shook my head.

"Well, that's a good start, at least. Most of your brain might well be intact! Before we can move on, though, I need you to do some reading. Through the written word comes elucidation, remember. It's all we have, the only authentic link to those that went before us, what they were thinking, how they really lived and felt."

He pulled out a slim volume from a pile at his feet.

"Here, read this and report back to me after the holiday. Sorry, I mean reading week."

The book was *The Swimming Pool Incident* by Nevile Thompson. A thin man with a heavy beard was on the cover walking along the side of a pool, wearing trunks; it looked as if it might have been painted by David Hockney in the 1970s.

"Funny spelling of Neville," I said.

"It's a pseudonym, I think, a bit of clever wordplay. When you read the story it might make more sense—the vile bit."

Monday, a week later

We had to hire a van because dad said he needed his for work. I put down a piece of carpet in the back and dotted pillows around.

"This vehicle's going to see some action," joked Al, rocking it gently.

"I'm not so sure," said Loachy, grinning.

Loachy sometimes didn't get the joke or see when people were sending themselves up.

The rain came down almost as soon as we set off. Snatches of sunshine broke through followed at regular intervals by downpours, as if on a pre-arranged basis.

"God is being vindictive on purpose," said Al. "Bit of sunshine, bit of rain. Bit of sunshine, lot of rain."

"Do you actually believe in God?" asked Loachy.

"Can we save that one until we're a few days in?" I asked.

On the first night Loachy stayed in the van, reading by torchlight. He had been telling us, at length, that he was going through a 'Primo Levi phase'. Al told him, come on, Primo wouldn't mind him having a night off from *The Drowned and the Saved*. He picked up the book and looked at the cover

104

featuring a photograph of prisoners at a concentration camp, presumably greeting their liberators, hands aloft and smiling.

"Look, Loachy, the lads are waving you off to the pub. I bet that lot were thirsty for a pint," said Al.

Theoretically, I had two girls but this often felt like none so I was happy to join Al on his 'trapping' missions (originally we used words such as 'trapping' as a piss-take of our parents—it was drawn from their vocabulary largely, along with 'birds' for girls, say, or 'courting' when you were going out with someone—but we did it now almost without any irony, a kind of affectation of being much older than we were).

Any girls we came across that night and the next few nights were usually playing pool in damp, near-empty, under-heated pubs with scrappy oilcloth on the floor. Most were with their boyfriends, chewing gum and pressing pudgy fingers into their phones, bored. 'Show village' girls were no more accessible than town girls. Al refused to believe they were actually from these villages and said they had probably travelled in from nearby council estates. One or two were at least approachable, four pints in.

"Hello, what's your name?"

"Why do you want to know?"

Al would shrug his shoulders, look down at the floor. We'd give in easily. We could talk all night about the paranormal; the films of Joel and Ethan Coen; astronomy; politics (specifically why it was weird to see Tony Blair shaking the hand of Colonel Gaddafi, which had been big news in the preceding weeks); the importance of *The Golden Bough* and its influence on mysticism; what was wrong (and right) with all our friends and everyone we knew and why they were like they were and where they might end up, in life. But we couldn't tell a pretty girl with dyed blonde hair and tight jeans why we wanted to know her name. Afterwards, on the walk back to the van, I'd rally.

"We've got a unique kind of charisma," I said. "It takes girls a while to see it, that's all. We're not shallow and superficial, so it means we're rubbish at small talk."

"You make us sound middle-aged," said Al.

"I think we *are* middle-aged, always have been. Since about the age of six anyway or whenever we first learned to think."

We walked in synchronisation for a short while, side by side.

"You've got Sarah, anyway," he said.

I told him I had and I hadn't, that I wasn't sure.

"That's why I'm here, sort of." I said. "To buy some time to think about what I want, where I'm going."

"What specifically?"

"Whether I want to be with Sarah. Whether I want to carry on at university. And all the Niall stuff has been getting me down."

Al was a great listener, capable of amazing empathy and sensitivity. I wondered how he'd respond to my candidness, my subtle plea for counsel. I heard a drum roll in my head. Here it comes.

"I'll never get a bird," he muttered.

The beer and the barrenness of the night had got to him, set him up for self-pity. I wondered: was he right—would he ever get a bird? Where were the girls who would fall for him? They definitely weren't playing pool on a Monday night in Grasmere, moaning that they were a bit cold, asking the landlord to put on another bar of the gas fire, please Bob. And then saying they didn't want any cheese and onion crisps because they were greasy last time and kept 'repeating'.

I guessed that the girls who might possibly be attracted to Al were backpacking round the world or away at university. Al had mucked about at school, so college wasn't an option and he didn't have the finance or fervour to travel. So he was stuck on a lonely wander around his hometown and imagination, stopping off sporadically to stare at the skies and consider the VY Canis Majoris, a star more than 2,000 times larger than the sun and 3,900 light years away from earth—as he'd tell you.

Perhaps Kizzy had been right, after all. Parking the van at night soon became an issue. Double yellow lines or 'controlled zones' were everywhere. If we parked on an avenue or crescent, busybody neighbours were soon staring from their window or standing on their doorsteps, much like Jack at home. Occasionally we'd see them shuffling up and down the pavement in their slippers, conferring with so-and-so from number thirty six. At last! All those hours they'd spent Neighbourhood Watching and, finally, a van and three strangers. One night, an old bloke tapped on the back doors. We'd just fallen asleep. Tap, tap, tap. Al pressed his face to the rear window.

"You can't park here, you know," said the man.

Al pushed the door open slightly.

"You can't park here, you know."

"How come?"

"Bylaws, it's in the bylaws. You can't park here, you know."

Most nights we'd end up on the car park of an industrial estate, though they were better known these days, we discovered, as enterprise zones or business parks. One morning, we were woken by crows padding on the roof.

"What time is it?"

"Nearly six."

Al said he couldn't sleep with all the noise and let himself out. He lit the portable gas stove, boiling water for cups of tea. It took ages. Me and Loachy stirred and sat up, our legs dangling over the bumper at the back of the van. The trees bordering the car park had come into leaf and were a striking yellow-green colour. Our breath was turning to steam but the sun was up and we could tell it was going to be a warm day, possibly without any drizzle. The stillness was splendid. The kettle came to the boil and Al served up three teas.

"This is the life," said Loachy, zipping up his trackie top and scanning a world that seemed all ours.

I put a CD into the player and a track came on that segued *Riders of the Storm* by The Doors into Blondie's *Rapture*. Al was intrigued.

"What's that?"

"It's called a mashup," said Loachy. "They've basically merged two sound files on a computer to make one song. There's no end to what's possible these days."

Loachy loved playing the role of teacher, delivering tablets of knowledge to the uninformed. He'd earlier briefed Al on 'blogging', explaining how the word had evolved from weblog and predicting that the concept might one day usurp books.

Al took a long slurp of tea and as it reached his belly sang: "Beautiful."

The word had barely left his lips when a police car drove up and parked parallel to the van, five or six metres away. The window on the driver's side came down.

"Does this vehicle belong to you?"

"It's borrowed."

"Borrowed?"

"From a hire company."

The window rose back up again while the copper spoke into his handset. A minute or so later the disappointment in his voice was palpable.

"It seems you're not telling fibs," he said. "You can't park here, though. Didn't you see the sign?"

"We'll finish these brews and get going," said Al.

"No you won't, you'll clear off now."

As we drove away, Al was furious.

"It's shit, isn't it? I mean, how big is England? And all we want is a quiet corner to park up in. Not much to ask."

"Don't let it get to you. It's what coppers do, hassle people," said Loachy.

We were hassled again, the next morning. We had parked on a dirt track off the main road. On waking, Al shinned down an embankment to a stream, past brambles and saplings tied to wooden staves. He was brushing his teeth when a police car appeared. The copper marched to the edge of the incline.

"Hey, you. What are you doing down there?"

Al turned round, mouth frothy with toothpaste.

"Brushing my teeth, what do you think I'm doing?"

"Get up here. Now."

The copper said he could arrest Al for being 'full of attitude'.

Afterwards, when we were driving, Al gave a heartfelt speech:

"This is what you get, total aggravation, when you try and do something a bit different, when you make a bid for freedom and don't go to work, come home and go to bed, all neat and tidy like the rest of this brain-dead fucking country."

We resolved to cut short the trip and head home. The decision seemed to make us more relaxed. A holiday, we'd each decided, especially one designated a 'Grand Tour', was probably best left as a fanciful dream, an ideal, and not actually effectuated. We had soon discovered that it wasn't picnics in churchyards with beautiful girls called Skye or Hermione or reciting poetry as we traversed breeze-brushed corn fields, but, instead, articulated lorries, service stations, clammy sandwiches, traffic jams and drizzle, lots of drizzle. And hostile police officers.

Loachy, ever the pragmatist, was well prepared for this anticlimax. He appeared so 'centred', in fact, as to view everything solely as an experience, probably later to be turned into art. For me, and more so, Al, the distance between our hoped-for, imagined selves, pre-holiday (free and easy, confident, inner city surfers lacking merely a surf board, bead necklaces and the sea) and our soon-discovered on-the-road selves (uptight, self-conscious and prone to moods) was as long as England, Grasmere to Boscastle—though we didn't actually get to Cornwall, nowhere near.

"Travel narrows the mind anyway," I said.

"Don't you mean broadens the mind?" said Loachy,

missing the facetiousness.

"No, narrows. You learn much more from being in one place all the time, travelling about in your head where it's warm and dry and there are no coppers to chase you around."

On the trip I'd noticed that Loachy had barely used his phone.

"Have you kept it touch with your harem?" I asked.

"What do you mean?" he said, forcing a laugh as if shocked by my effrontery.

"Ladies one, two and three."

"We don't do messaging. We make arrangements and we stick to them. Life is simple."

"Do you know what I really don't like?" asked Al, unprompted. "Women on dating sites who go on about how well-travelled they are or how they've lived abroad and it's 'shaped them'. They're running away from something, I reckon."

"Themselves," I said.

After we'd each admitted taking sneaky or, occasionally, lingering looks on such sites, we began listing off-putting things we'd seen on them. I was surprised Loachy contributed. He must have considered it a holiday from his routine non-discriminatory, non-sexist, non-fun self. The list included: women who said they were curvaceous or curvy when they were overweight (Al); women whose profile photograph had been done professionally after a makeover job (Loachy); women with hippy tag-names such as Moonshine or Flower Child (Al); women who listed salsa or flamenco dancing as a hobby (Al); women who claimed to be 'free-spirited' or 'intuitive' (me); women who loved romcoms (Loachy); women who, on their profile shot, clearly had a bloke (possibly two) standing next to them but had clumsily photoshopped them off (Al); women who described themselves as 'ditzy' or 'high maintenance' (Loachy); women who referred to men as 'guys' (me); women wearing outdoorsy clothing on their photo—ski pants, padded anoraks, gloves etc (Al); women who pouted (Loachy); women with dyed blonde hair who banged on about not being typically 'blonde' (i.e.: stupid) (Al); women in bandanas, berets or almost any type of headwear (me); women holding up wine glasses or, worse, drinking from pint pots (Al); women who claimed to love walking and the countryside but hardly ever left their houses, where they read magazines about walking and the countryside (Loachy).

"Do you think we're a bit fussy?" I asked.

"No," they chorused.

I asked Al what he *did* like, then. He answered immediately:

"Women who wear tight necklaces on their pictures or lean forward showing off a bit of cleavage, or, better still, a lot of cleavage."

"What about you, Loachy?"

"The eyes and the smile tell you everything you need to know, man."

"Hippy," scoffed Al.

After a few seconds of silence, Al said:

"I might go on that Friends Reunited site when I get home. That's got to be a good way of checking out who is available and who is married off. And you already know them from way back, so you've not got to go through all the introducing yourself bollocks."

At that point a car came up close behind and then overtook us, racing off.

"Cunt," shouted Loachy.

"Where's he going in such a hurry?" I asked.

"A bland semi, his boring wife, a crappy meal, kids he hates," said Loachy.

"Perhaps that's one thing we've learned on this cock-up of a trip," said Al.

"What's that?" asked Loachy.

"That we're us, not them, and being us is usually okay."

"Intense!" shouted Loachy.

I dropped off the van at the hire company and walked home with three plastic bags stuffed with cushions, a rucksack over my shoulder. Mum answered the door. I noticed dad wasn't around.

"He's upstairs," she said.

"Upstairs?"

"Yes, upstairs," she answered, sounding peeved.

"How come?"

"He's been there most of the time since he heard about Niall."

Dad was always first up in the morning. He hated malingerers.

"I shouldn't have mentioned the word 'leukaemia'—that's what set him off," she said. "I should have been vague like the bloody doctors, not sure what day it is half the time."

While I'd been away Jenny had surfed the internet and

found out all she could about the variants of leukaemia—acute myeloid leukaemia, chronic myeloid leukaemia and, worse still in this gallery of crude and ugly words: acute lymphoblastic leukaemia. The more she read, the more she believed she stood a better chance of defeating it. She told us that Niall probably had acute lymphoblastic leukaemia because it mainly afflicted kids. She had all the facts: it was a cancer of the marrow found in the cavities of the body's longer bones. Six thousand people were treated for it each year in Britain. She began writing everything down assiduously and didn't hear when we said he might not have leukaemia, it might be something else, a something that could be more easily cured.

Thursday

Jenny phoned late at night in a panic. She had gone to check on Niall before turning in. As she leaned over the bed to kiss his cheek in the darkness, she felt dampness. She thought at first it was sweat or he'd knocked over a glass of water. She dabbed his face with her finger and put it to her mouth. It was blood. She switched on the bedside light and saw a red halo around his head. He'd had a nosebleed. She woke him and washed him down, trying hard not to make him sense her alarm. She said later that this was the moment she decided: she had to find out definitively what was wrong with him.

After she'd cleaned him up she went to bed but was unable to sleep. She got up and walked around the house, her mind on ice. She did the ironing—his tops with bears on them and cartoon characters, pressing down on Spider-Man, Batman and fluffy lions dressed in football kits. She held them to her face, feeling the soft warmth on her cheeks. She said it was the longest night of her life. Finally, the street lights fizzed out and daylight moved through the town. She willed everyone to open their curtains, start the day.

She had to wait until midmorning before the consultant was able to take her phone call.

"He's had a nosebleed," she told him. "The pillow was completely soaked."

He told her children often had acute nosebleeds.

"I've known them fill a bucket or two," he joked.

He asked how Niall had been since the nosebleed. He'd seemed his usual self, Jenny told him.

"That's good," he said. "If he has bleeds two or three times this week and it's heavy each time, please book an appointment with my secretary. I promise I will see him."

I'd had an idea while driving through the rain to Dunster, or was it Lower Slaughter? I was going to conduct a near-scientific study of my relationship with Sarah, specifically focused on how much she loved me, or didn't. There were two ideal topics—Niall's illness and the abandoned road trip. How much would Sarah ask about both and therefore reveal her interest in me and my life? How long, in minutes spent, would our conversation linger on these subjects? And how would that contrast, time wise, to stuff *she* brought up? If we're to go even deeper: how would she fare if compared to Kate? Who cared for me and loved me the most? I knew, even as I did the maths, that this was all pitiful and no real way to gauge anything, probably.

I phoned Sarah and we arranged to have a drink. On the drive to the bar she asked about the trip but I fended her off. I didn't want any possibility of us being interrupted by the radio or traffic—it might affect the scientific nature of the analysis.

"I'll tell you later."

"Oh goody," she said, assuming this meant I was teasing her and had some amazing news to relate.

In the bar she forgot for a good while to return to the subject. She talked instead about her friend's new boyfriend called James who was 'a bit of a bore'; how her mum was doing without her dad, better than expected, actually; how busy she was at work, snowed under; how lazy Ben was—I wondered whether this was designed to sprinkle pepper on any tracks that might lead me to discover they were having an affair (I realised that by being away I'd given her a good opportunity to be with him); a film she wanted to see [*Man on Fire*] starring Denzel Washington that was 'supposed to be brilliant' and a comprehensive rundown of what she had watched on television the previous evening [*Shameless*, followed by a new programme called *Strictly Come Dancing* and then a 'good-ish' crime drama, *The Brief*]. Did all this quick-quick talking mean she wanted to share, wanted to love, and was this flattering to me, being so close to her life, or was it her self-obsession played out for its own sake? She finally remembered:

116

"Sorry, I forgot to ask how it went with Loachy and Al. Do tell."

"Well, as you know, we barely got to any of the places we planned to."

She nodded. Was she going to ask any supplementary questions? Didn't look like it. I carried on, telling her about the run-ins with police, the daft things Al had been saying, his non-PC views on women.

"Sounds like an adventure."

Was that her best shot? *Sounds like an adventure*. Didn't she want any more? How I felt? Who we met—girls, perhaps? Would she reveal any signs of jealousy?

"I thought it would be more of an adventure to be honest," I said. "And it felt a bit weird not being at home after what had happened with Niall [she clearly wasn't going to ask about him so I had no alternative but to lead her there]."

She leaned forward. I told her about the nosebleed and how we were all wiped out with worry.

"It's all so awful," she said.

The expression sounded paltry but what else could she say to reflect the true magnitude? We moved on to other things, chatting happily, and my experiment no longer seemed to matter. Afterwards I wondered if I had invalidated it from the start by rebuffing her first inquiry about the trip, asking her to wait until later. Also, while I was away, there had been dozens of texts between us, so it wasn't as if she had been starved of information, or me, for any length of time.

*

117

Sunday

On the night before I was due back at university I read the book Joe had given me. It had the feel of one of those curious and laboured foreign films from Eastern Europe. The story featured a man who visited his local swimming baths at the same time every Tuesday evening. He lived alone and had a mundane life: goes to work (car park attendant, doing crosswords and word puzzles in a tiny hut), has an evening meal, watches television, goes to bed. The focus of his week is the Tuesday swim. Eventually it turns out that he is gay and has developed a crush on a boy of 'about sixteen' who attends the baths with a group of 'rowdy' friends.

After many *Lolita*-inspired pages of yearning for this boy, containing near-forensic detail—down to the creases in his swimming trunks and numerous mentions of the hairline at the nape of his neck—the protagonist's lucky day arrives. While he is drying himself in the changing rooms, the boy enters with a cut knee; he has caught it on the edge of the diving board. The man tells him he is a doctor and asks him to sit on a bench and raise his leg. Across about ten pages heavy in metaphor and allegory, he describes how he tends the wound, basically getting off on touching this lad but in such a way that would not necessarily pass as inappropriate or sexual. Afterwards the narration suggests that this encounter will sate him for the rest of his life; he has reached nirvana.

Monday

I arrived early at university and went to the refectory. As I entered I saw the Goldsmiths, Lana and Esther, sitting at a table by the entrance. I had spoken to them a few times but it was one of those situations where to sit with them felt a bit familiar but to sit elsewhere would have looked standoffish. I poured myself a coffee and moved towards them.

"Anyone's seat?" I asked.

"No," said Lana.

They were near-identical twin daughters of an ophthalmologist who, in tribute to their dad, wore glasses with ultra-thick lenses. They were sharp minded, had long hair and wore tight jeans. In one of Joe's first lectures they revealed that they were members of the Conservative Party. Joe joked with them about the leader of the party, Michael Howard, being 'one of their gang'.

"What do you mean?" asked Esther.

"His real name is Michael Hecht. He's a Rumanian Jew. There's a lot of you lot about, you know, walking those corridors of power."

"Isn't that racist?"

"I think you'll find that it's a truism which means it can't be racist, surely."

Joe was big on politics and, true to form, extremely left-wing. The Goldsmiths were a convenient target and he hammered them routinely as if they were the embodiment of every staid, traditionalist, monetarist value that underpinned the evil, horrible, fetid state. He especially had it in for Lana because she'd sighed loudly in the very first lecture when he began ranting about Sinclair, the university vice-chancellor. Another time he had been going off, screaming for the revolution, piling up the profanities, when she interrupted.

"Are you supposed to be doing this? Isn't it against the rules?"

"What rules?"

"University rules."

"Rules are there to be broken."

She shook her head.

"This isn't on," she said. "All the preaching you're doing. You're supposed to be teaching us creative writing not the fucking *Communist Manifesto*."

It was good that she had sworn. One of her fucks was worth twenty of his, an atom bomb after all the hand grenades. Go on Lana, give him some more. She did. It was brilliant.

"I wouldn't mind but everything you say is so stereotypical. It's as if you're stuck in the 1960s with all this corny rhetoric. It doesn't mean anything. It's hackneyed. We're all about twenty five years younger than you, at least. And we've heard it all before, everyone has."

Half way through her speech he'd started grinning. He asked if she'd finished her 'little outburst'.

"No, one more thing," she said. "Why are you flouncing around college indoctrinating us and not out there in the real world? Is it because we're considered easy—a pushover?"

"You've been got, Lana, thinking I'm the enemy," he said. "When I'm patently not the fucking enemy. The enemy is all around you but invisible to you. They've been getting at you since you were born, in insidious ways."

Sitting together now, sipping strong coffee, the time felt right to commend Lana.

"I've been meaning to say this for ages. That outburst when you blasted Joe, it was fantastic."

I was going to tell her about his study and what he had said to me there and the book he'd given me but she snapped:

"He's a fuck-up."

She was playing with the sleeve of her jumper, stretching it and wrapping loose threads at the cuff tightly around her fingers.

"What do you mean?" I asked.

She said Joe's dad had been a major or captain or something big in the army. He'd never really cared about his kids and treated them as if they were his platoon. They had to clean their shoes until they could see their reflection in them and were beaten if they were naughty. This was why Joe had such a big issue with authority and was fixated with people such as Sinclair.

"How do you know all this?" I asked.

"My dad had a receptionist who worked for him years ago who went to the same school as he did."

I'd never thought before of Joe having a life outside university. He was so much part of it. I suddenly wondered: what did he do at night? Where did he go? I'd never imagined him having parents or brothers and sisters, though, come to think of it, hadn't he mentioned a brother fishing with him at Brixham? Until Lana's revelation, I'd thought charismatic rebels merely existed, on their own, not needing the things the rest of us sought: family, lovers, somewhere to live, friends. The information about his dad changed everything. It was the first time I'd properly looked at someone from round the back, their history, to see them more clearly. I'd always assumed the anger of clever people was righteous too, borne from the injustice they saw around them and not because they came from a dysfunctional family or as a consequence of something that had happened to them years before.

"Another thing," said Esther. "Don't you think he's a bit effeminate?"

"Isn't he married?" I asked.

"Divorced."

"But he's sort of macho," I said. "You know—mentally strong, opinionated. I'm struggling for the words here..."

"I'll give you one," said Esther. "Faggy"

"Is there anything wrong with that?" I asked.

"I mean he's faggy creepy not, like, faggy gay, which is totally cool."

Joe gave a lecture that morning on 'how to grow stories'. He was on good form, even having banter with Barry and the Goldsmith girls.

"How's my fan club this morning?" he asked, waving his forefinger as if zapping them with a gun.

I was pondering on how he was going to approach me about the Nevile Thompson book. He barely made eye contact until the very end when he slipped me a piece of paper; it seemed unnecessarily furtive. 'Meet me at my den at 1pm'. After what Esther had said and the subject matter of the book, I was beginning to wonder.

"What did Joe hand you?"

I hadn't realised that anyone had noticed. It was Adam Birtles, a bloke in his mid-thirties who had started the course after leaving his job as a reporter on a local newspaper. Much the same as me, he didn't fit the profile of the rest of the students. Most of the others were from the south-east, private or grammar school educated and, in easy classification, from artsy middle-class backgrounds. He was wide in build and attitude. His mouth was open perpetually, whether speaking or not. He had fashioned a little tuft of hair at the front of his head which looked like a squashed Shredded Wheat. Most days he wore flower patterned shirts and old fashioned bootcut jeans. I wondered whether the university had a clandestine policy of selecting oddballs like Birtles and Barry to counter the prevailing stereotype, perhaps in the hope they could write as eccentrically as they dressed and acted. Birtles had spoken to me only once before, to claim he had slept with a glamour model. I joked that I had, too. Several. At the same time.

"No, seriously. I met her in a nightclub," he'd said. "Down in Essex somewhere. I tell you, she was one randy lady. I was dipping my dick in warm salty water for weeks afterwards. Red raw it was."

I'd last heard the word 'randy' about twenty years earlier in a dim-witted sitcom.

As I left the lecture theatre, he followed me closely.

"Has he invited you out on a date?" asked Birtles.

"Not quite."

"He wants to watch it," he averred. "It can be a very contentious matter that, over-fraternising with students."

I turned to face him, not sure what to say. I saw that he had a black eye and was missing a front tooth. Before I could ask, he said:

"I had a fight in the chicken shop last night. This bloke lamped me straight in the smacker. Took my tooth clean out."

"Did he then hit you in the eye?"

"He did, actually. Straight in. Pop! Couldn't see a thing."

He said he was planning to take his assailant to court and was hopeful of a decent compensation pay-out. He was going to the Caribbean on the proceeds. The girls were already waiting for him by the pool, he said. He swerved the conversation back to Joe.

"Is he a gay?" he asked.

"I don't know."

"Are you a gay?"

"No, I'm not *a* gay," I said, mocking him slightly (which he didn't notice).

"I thought not," he said.

Joe's study was chilly and I rubbed my hands together as I entered.

"There's been no heating on over the break," he said. "A ruse by Sinclair, no doubt, to save as much money as possible. Keep the overlords happy and all that. Useless and heartless, two for the price of one in the same man. Imagine that!"

I sat in the armchair.

"Well then, did you read old Nevile's masterpiece?" he asked.

"I did."

"What did you think?"

"I liked it."

(I don't know why I'd said this because I hadn't, really. I felt under pressure to be positive because he'd called it a masterpiece and he seemed in such a good mood, smiling away).

"Tell me more."

"I liked the use of language and sense of control."

"A bit, you know, slow, though, wouldn't you say?"

Joe had detected my reservations, presumably from my facial expressions or body language. Truth time.

"Yeah, very slow," I said. "And weird."

"Weird?"

"Yes, weird, but not in a good way."

He cocked an ear and smiled.

"I'm not sure I know what you mean."

"It's a forced weird as if the writer wants you to think he's weird. And it's an unsettling weird. There's something else going on under the surface that's not actually in the text but subliminal."

He lent back in his chair:

"Deep."

I continued:

"It left me feeling unnerved, how the protagonist is actually a bit seedy and sneaky but you sort of root for him and don't

125

want him to get found out."

"Isn't that a skill, being able to summon moral ambiguity?"

"Ambiguity is easy to achieve. It's much harder to give your characters a moral code, to work within accepted boundaries rather than filling your books with oddballs and mavericks."

As I was speaking, giving it to him straight, his face did something I'd never seen a face do before. It looked as if it was made of wax and a fire had been lit beneath it. Slowly, the features fell, his eyes becoming wide. And then I remembered: moral ambiguity, assailing your sensibilities—this was precisely Joe's plan for the (literary) world. The book was his own personal manifesto laid bare, in subject matter and style, everything he was and believed in. And here I was, trampling it underfoot. My thoughts suddenly hit a red light and were colliding into each other. The final one, which I should have had two weeks earlier when the book was so blithely thrown in my direction, was that Joe *was* Nevile Thompson; they were the same person.

I heard a sound. It was Joe's pager fixed to his belt. I didn't know pagers still existed. I felt as if I was waking from a dream.

"It's reception," he said. "I'll have to get over there."

"Do you want me to wait?"

His face was back to normal.

"Probably not a good idea. I don't know how long I'm going to be. Let's leave it for now."

Wednesday

Without Andrew to share the attention, life at John and Joan's became even more intense. I was putting on weight because of the gargantuan meals. Princess was too because I constantly passed food to her under the table; I had to get rid of it somehow. I had told them about Niall and they asked about him almost every day.

One night, Joan said she was off to bed, 'with Dan'.

"I'm going to spend an hour with him," she joked.

As soon as she left the room John looked at me and then the door, making sure she'd gone.

"She's reading that bloody awful book, *The Da Vinci Code*. He's a crossword addict, you know, that Dan Brown."

John was always proffering bits of random information. He didn't surf the internet so I wasn't sure from where it was appropriated.

"It's sold millions, that book," he said. "That's what I read in *Reader's Digest* at the barber's last week."

I left it a few seconds to presage a change of subject.

"I've got a bit of woman trouble," I volunteered.

As soon as the sentence left my lips I regretted saying it. John reached for the remote and jabbed excitedly, turning down the volume. He pushed up his glasses. I thought he might even be about to twang the shoulder strap of his off-white vest.

"What kind of woman trouble?"

I told him how I was unsure about Sarah, whether it was meant to be, and about meeting Kate.

"What's she like, this Kate?"

"She's a nice girl."

"Shapely?"

"I suppose so, yes."

"Does she make your ears pop?"

He'd used this expression before in relation to glamour model he'd seen in *The Sun*. Andrew would have backed off at this point, feigning to be affronted by such crudeness and invasion of privacy. I didn't fancy a night sleeping in the car or a two hour drive home.

"I suppose she does, yes."

"Really? Stick with her then, I would."

"You've got to talk to them at some point!" I said.

"That's what you've got mates for. Talk to them, instead. I always think it's best to be with a woman who gets your sap rising. You'll stand anything if you continually want to tup them, though they can drive you bastard mad if they're forever flirting with other blokes. You see, I made a mistake with Joan. She's a lovely woman, don't get me wrong, and a good companion but, God bless her, she's not the prettiest flower in the garden, is she, especially now she's chubbed up. If you're not engaged down below, you soon start to get bored and that's when the bickering starts, like with us two arguing over nowt most of the time."

He stopped talking for a few seconds. He'd had what he thought was a good idea:

"Why don't you keep both girls on the go? You're a young lad—make the most of it."

"I can't do that, John. I'm not cut out for it. I think about things too much."

"You want to watch that. Doesn't do any bugger any good, fretting."

Thursday

Whenever I spoke to mum on the phone she mentioned how badly dad had been affected by Niall's illness. He had given up on restraint and blurted out whatever he was thinking about his grandson, unable to veil his anger and fatalism. Mum didn't actually say it directly but I could tell she thought a man-to-man, son-to-dad summit might help. I decided to cut short the week at university and return home.

"Is that allowed?" she asked. "You're hardly ever there."

I told her it was the modern way, that most courses involved just a few hours of lectures each week and, being a creative writing course, I was supposed to spend a lot of the time reading and writing.

"I don't really see the point of you being there, then" she said.

It was a fair comment.

Soon after I arrived home, mum excused herself and went into the kitchen. At least dad was up and out of bed, even if he looked terrible.

"Mum tells me you're not dealing with all this Niall stuff very well." I said.

"You know what's going to happen, don't you?" he said gravely. "He'll get more and more ill and then he'll die. A little

129

kid like that. Dead. How are we supposed to deal with that?"

"Dad, he's going to be okay."

"He's not. He's going to die."

He shook his head.

"What kind of God does something like this?"

"You've not got to think or talk like that."

"I know that, I know that," he said, annoyed. "But there are some things you can't control, things you can't stay calm and collected about. You can't. A life getting started and then stamped out. It isn't fair."

Hunched on the settee, he looked small and vulnerable.

"Dad, just try, will you? For all our sakes."

"I'll do my best."

"What are they saying at work?"

"They've said I can have off as much time as I want."

"That's probably not a good thing. What have you told them you've got wrong with you?"

"I've got depression—the doctor has given me a note confirming it."

"You, depressed? You've scoffed at people with depression before now."

I waited for him to say something but he didn't.

I went to my room and sat on the edge of the bed. The transformation in dad's personality was alarming; so strong and dependable for all those years but now turned inside out, exposed. Mum was disappointed by his collapse, made angry by his lack of support. Everyone had to be strong for Niall, she said, to carry on as normal, swallow down hard the worry.

(You have this idea about serious illness, that certain people and families are prepared somehow, marked out for it, so there is a notion of it belonging to them. But it's not like that. Illness is arbitrary. It lands, splat, like something fallen from the sky into your path. Everything is then changed, the future uncertain, your confidence obliterated. I understood dad's response. He was of a generation of steel and stone, well tethered until this dread and disappointment had become too much to bear—the possible suffering and then loss of a kid who was so funny and lively as to define life itself.)

A week later

Niall didn't have any more nosebleeds. He was still back and forward to the hospital but most of the time he looked so well that you had to remind yourself he was ill. One of the tests involved taking a sample from his bone marrow, inserting a needle and drawing it out. Jenny described it and it made me feel sick.

I took him out for a couple of walks. Jenny said not to tire him but he didn't show signs of slowing. Up and over hills, no trouble. Throwing stones in reservoirs. Challenging me to fights with fern stems. All the time, asking questions I couldn't answer.

"What's that there? Why is that like that?"

We set fire to a small patch of bracken, him jumping up and down in excitement. I tore off a branch from a pine tree to make a sparkler, lighting it so it fizzed and smelled of sweet sap.

"Whooaagh, look at those flames."

"Is this allowed?" he asked,

"Not really," I said. "But as long as we don't set the whole place on fire, we'll be okay."

High on the moors we walked along a path beside a reservoir. Only a few trees had found a footing and flourished at such altitude, buffeted by cold winds. A mile or so further on, we found an abandoned car. While I was working out how it had got there and for how long it had been rusting into the soil, Niall cocked his little legs over the bonnet and clambered on to the roof. My instinct was to tell him to be careful or even admonish him but I kept quiet. I was proud that he'd done just what he wanted to do. He looked about him, past the circle of rosebay willowherb to the moors on all sides, king of the world.

Saturday

The news came through while I was home, the letter arriving at Jenny's on a Saturday morning. Niall didn't have leukaemia, after all. He had anaemia, an illness that sounded familiar and homespun in comparison. Mum and dad said they'd known people who were anaemic, kids from their school, pale things who'd gone somewhere for a few weeks (the countryside, probably) and come back singing and dancing. Almost as if by giving his condition a different name, he had been cured, near enough. And dad's depression melted in a heartbeat.

It wasn't the anaemia mum and dad knew, however. This version was aplastic anaemia. Jenny was back on the internet. Niall's bone marrow wasn't producing enough blood cells which meant his body lacked oxygen and his blood wasn't able to clot properly, making him susceptible to infection.

Dad wanted to know how this had happened, what had caused it. No one was sure; it was difficult to say for definite. It might have been hereditary or triggered by an earlier illness. The consultant asked Jenny whether Niall had ever had lupus or hepatitis. He hadn't. He said that in seventy five per cent of cases they didn't know why it occurred. Dad wouldn't give up on speculating.

"Uncle Harry, my dad's brother, he had a bit of trouble with his blood."

The exercise was pointless really because as much as we considered Niall entirely our own, he was one-half Simon and we knew next to nothing about his family. Dad announced this as if he'd made a great discovery (when the rest of us had thought of it already):

"Bloody hell, I bet it's that lot. They were all like little shivery ghosts, weren't they? Simon wasn't nine stones wet through."

The letter revealed that Niall had the mildest of the three versions of the condition—non-severe aplastic anaemia. He was prescribed tablets to stimulate the bone marrow and help produce cells. If this failed, he'd need occasional blood transfusions, hormone injections and courses of antibiotics. At the very worst he'd need a bone marrow transplant. Jenny was given a card outlining things he should avoid—visits to the dentist (in case he bled), uncooked food, contact sports, plane travel, construction sites.

"Is that a joke?" asked dad. "The bit about construction sites."

"No. Some sites can be a source of a certain type of fungi that might affect him," she said.

"I've worked in building all my life but I've never heard of that before."

Sunday

Jenny visited with Niall. Dad asked him if he was allergic to museums because the three of us—me, him and Niall—were going to have a 'lads' day out' at an aircraft museum. This was news to me but dad was so jolly I couldn't resist.

Before we set off Kate called on my mobile. She'd never done this before; I'd always contacted her. I could hear my heartbeat in my ears. She began chatting, asking how I was and saying she was a bit tired (she made a yawning sound) and wasn't sure what to do with the rest of the day, whether she should visit her friend Laura who had just had a baby, a lovely little lad called Rory with big blue eyes, or stay in and pamper herself. Abruptly, she asked why I hadn't taken her out lately.

"I've been tied up," I said.

"Sounds interesting. Did it hurt?"

"What?"

"The tying up."

"No."

"Well it's not worth doing then, is it?"

It was corny stuff but it got me every time and made me want to see her, have sex with her. I said I'd call her in a day or two, sort something out. As I pressed down on the phone, I imagined I wasn't just turning it off but shutting her out, cauterising a part of my life that wasn't supposed to be happening.

Niall was excited about seeing the planes grandad had told him about many times — Halifaxes, Spitfires, Lancaster Bombers. The museum was based at a foggy disused airfield in the middle of nowhere. An old boy in uniform was at the entrance gates. He came haring out of his little wooden hut as if we were the first visitors for weeks. His eyes sparkled when he saw Niall on the back seat. He implored him to open the window, quickly, quickly, so he could pass through a handful of rolled up posters and postcards.

"You can have these, completely free. I've been hoping a junior wing commander would visit us today."

Niall blushed.

"What do you say, Niall?"

"Thank you," he whispered.

It wasn't really a place for children but designed more for aviation enthusiasts. Half-assembled planes were dotted around the airfield or roped off in hangers. There was a strong smell of oil and spray paint. Many of the exhibits were sections of engine laid on the asphalt floor with typewritten notes explaining the intricacies of how they were engineered. A sign on a wall said: 'Pilots this way' and pointed to a cockpit propped up on scaffolding. Inside the plane, the roof was very low and dad told Niall at least three times to be careful. Bang, he hit his head on a lever hanging down. Dad tutted. Niall bit his lip to stop himself crying. I rubbed his forehead. He told me to get off, it didn't hurt.

Huts that had provided accommodation for air crews in the Second World War were full of glass cases containing old uniforms and kit bags. Dummies in RAF uniforms were propped up against walls. They were covered in dirt, their noses and ears chipped off, eyes staring out spookily. An ancient wooden speaker relayed scratchy commentary about the war in a posh voice. You could feel the past; it was in the woodwork, seeped into the bricks. The whole place was damp and dreary and fantastic.

Niall began coughing and dad made a fuss, asking whether we should see if the souvenir shop sold scarves and hats, fretting that we should have wrapped him up better. He found a toffee stuck to paper in his coat pocket and disgorged it into Niall's hand. It looked as old as some of the exhibits.

"Here, suck on this, it'll do you the world of good."

Niall popped it in his mouth. I noticed dad resting his hand on Niall's shoulder as he passed him the sweet. A small gesture but it cut me up. I had to look away into the mist, towards the spindly trees standing in rows across the airfield.

The café was in another hut. They were serving roast beef and Yorkshire pudding. The staff looked to be made up of kids on work placement schemes and pensioner volunteers. Dad persuaded Niall to have lots of gravy, telling him it would put hair on his chest and stop him coughing, too.

"How does it do that, grandad?"

"It gets into the tubes and gives them a good soaking. Just what they need."

Niall seemed convinced. He turned to me:

"Did you know that?"

I said I didn't but grandad knew more about the power of gravy than I did.

The souvenir shop was in a narrow building made from breezeblocks with a corrugated tin roof. An elderly woman sat on a stool behind the counter, knitting. A notebook was in front of her in which she'd written the day's sales, four or five in a neat line, the prices aligned meticulously beneath one another. The shop stocked books by local authors about their wartime experiences, full of spelling mistakes. How they were sad times but defanately enjoyible too because everyone pulled together and made the most of it. Niall wanted a homemade teddy bear in a flying outfit but I think dad thought it was a bit cissy. He bought him a model airplane instead and said they could put it together when they got home. Niall was pleased enough and said as we were walking out:

"I'm a bit old for teddies now, aren't I?"

We set off and had been driving for a short while when dad told me how it took him back, all this.

"Only seems five minutes ago when I was coming to places like this with you, when you were a nipper. It's crazy how time flies. It goes like that [he clicked his fingers]."

He had the look of someone who had been swindled and couldn't work out how it had happened. I fell disconsolate, realising my life was going to be the same as his, as everybody else's: so quickly gone. It was the first time I could remember it being the three of us on our own, three generations together, me in the middle, shuffling towards the precipice that dad could now see over. I was then thinking about what he'd said. I couldn't recall trips to museums or many days out when I was a kid. I didn't say anything. No point in spoiling the mood.

Dad began assembling the model as soon as we got home. I could tell Niall was getting on his nerves with his clumsy attempts to help, squeezing the glue too hard and passing him the wrong bits of kit.

"He's being really short in there with him," I told Jenny who was washing up in the kitchen.

"What do you expect?"

I shrugged. I think I expected him to be different with Niall after getting so distraught and worried that we might lose him. To have changed, softened. I realised he couldn't help himself, couldn't become what he wasn't; no one can.

Monday

As everyone filed into the lecture theatre Joe pointed at me and said breezily:

"One o'clock, my study. Is it a date?"

I don't know how this happened but as I scanned the faces around me I immediately settled upon Birtles. His mouth was open even more than usual.

"He *is* a gay, isn't he?"

"Honest, Adam, I don't know."

I noticed that the swelling around his eye had gone down and the bruising had faded. His smile was still missing a tooth, though.

"Feeling better?" I asked.

"I am but I won't be going to the Caribbean, no way."

"How come?"

He told me he had appeared in court and been found guilty of 'fighting behaviour'. I said I'd never heard of such an offence.

"It's a very old one, left over on the bill of statutes," he said. "I've got to say, this fella's solicitor was brilliant. He made it sound as if I'd stormed into the fried chicken place shouting at everyone and bragging about how my shirt had cost more than they all earned in a week."

"Maybe the way you look doesn't help," I said.

"How do you mean?"

"You know, a bit smart, clothes-wise, for around here, anyway."

"You might be right, you know. They were probably jealous. Got to say though, the solicitor was amazing: a-maz-ing. He was so good at making me out to be the bad guy in it all."

He moved away, down a few steps and across to the side. I hadn't noticed Cardigan Barry next to me. He was shaking his head:

"How much of a dick is he? What's he even doing here?"

After the lecture Joe welcomed me into his study extravagantly, holding out his arm and gesturing as I waited at the door.

"Step this way, young man."

He asked me to sit down. He paced the room like a regular Sherlock, as if he was playing a role but in a knowingly hammy way. At any moment I expected him to make a dastardly aside to the audience.

"So, Nevile Thompson," he said. "Ne-Vile, a man of bile among the cubicles and the chlorine, a predatory pederast with paedophilia on his mind, possibly."

"The character was a fictional creation," I said. "Nevile himself might have been a fine and decent man, and, quite probably, a heterosexual."

"Or perhaps a fine and decent heterosexual with a predilection for homoerotic scheming played out through the characters in his books."

"That did cross my mind."

"I dare say it did," he said. He then pouted and I nearly shot upright because the mannerism was so camp. The Goldsmiths were right. And Birtles. He was *a* gay, surely.

"Anyhows," he said, shaking his head as if rubbing away all he'd said before. "I've not brought you here to discuss nefarious Nevile, if indeed that is his real name."

He pointed at the bookcases.

"This lot, do you think they'd be published these days?"

I scanned the spines.

"Pick any you want," he said.

I noticed a seam of Christopher Isherwood novels.

"Christopher Isherwood."

"No chance."

"Why not?"

"Too slow. They'd say nothing happens. Who'd buy him? Choose another."

"Alberto Moravia."

"Ah, dear old Alberto, a pornographer of distinction. A man who could work a rhapsody around the lifting of the hem of a skirt or the look thrown from wife to husband as they unpacked their swimming gear on the beach. Sorry Alberto, no room at the inn. Where to place you, old friend. To which genre do you belong? Perhaps if you spiced it up a bit and told us markedly less of the human condition and sexed it up big style, who knows?"

I was going to choose another.

"Anyway, you get the point," he said. "What I'm saying is that literature as we have known it, so shall it be in the end, is dead. Dead, dead, dead. Not the type of thing I should be telling a budding, bright-eyed student, I know, but you brought it up."

I didn't know I had. I must have looked puzzled.

"Come on, when you did your speech about how you hated magic realism and books about acrobats and talking dogs. You're the one who put all this in my head."

I didn't understand the link.

"Not so long ago you could *indulge*," he said. "It was an important aspect of being a writer. You were allowed the luxury of creative whimsy. Now, you have to write for a pre-existing market and it's a commercial one with no consideration of originality or invention. Writers back then were different.

They had character and charisma and this lifted them above the bloodless automotons of this world, the likes of Sinclair and his box-ticking, form-filling cronies."

"Are you saying this because you're not published anymore?"

"Of course I am but that's not reductive to my argument, it strengthens it. I still have something to say. Books of mine like *The Aftermath* and *Until I Close My Eyes* were supposed to be snapshots—you know, constituents of a much larger collection of work. I still write, most days in here, for a couple of hours at least. I shut that door and get on with it. Habitually it's middling but I might get one day a month, at best, where I transcend mediocrity and go home reasonably happy with what I've done. The rest is a slog; a slow, tedious slog like shovelling coal. And what for, what's it for? It used to be because I believed someone was reading, sharing, that someone cared. But they don't. It's like shouting down an empty cave or looking in the mirror and not seeing a reflection. Do you know how frightening that can be? How it can send you mad?"

Spittle was on his bottom lip. He brushed it away with his long chubby forefinger and took a breath. I thought he was about to cry. He pressed on:

"Do you plan to write in a particular genre?"

Before I could answer he began speaking again.

"You'd better do! Give them anything outside of an easily identifiable niche and they're fucked. So what does the poor old writer do? He sells his soul, of course. He writes what has already been written, rearranged slightly. He opts for the demands of editors and marketing departments rather than doing his own best work, what he really believes in. Give him a theme, a title, a cover, and he'll do the rest. They're only words. What way round would you like them? Long and philosophical, densely knitted or cool and terse, any way you like. Listen, I know this sounds like a fucking speech. That's because it is a speech and it's one I want you to hear."

He looked out of the window. He didn't say anything for about twenty seconds. The trees were swaying slightly. I could hear cars passing in the distance. When he did speak, it was so quiet I had to ask him to repeat it.

"I think that's it for today, more than enough."

Niall complained that some kids had been picking on him at school. Jenny said he didn't seem to have many friends and was a bit of a loner. He'd told her one of the dinner ladies had shouted at him for wandering around on his own in the playground.

"Find yourself a friend. Everyone else has one," she'd said.

Another time, the same woman caught him in the cloak room, sitting in a corner.

"Get out there," she ordered.

Jenny was furious but didn't complain. Niall had begged her not to.

"She'll pick on me more, then," he said.

Jenny believed his illness had made him shy and quiet. She told me that when she'd tried to persuade him to mix with classmates, he'd said to her solemnly:

"You don't know what children are like—they're cruel."

Jenny hadn't known what to say to him. She asked me to find out more:

"He'll talk to you. You know what it's like to be a boy."

Niall was matter-of-fact when I asked.

"They kick me in the leg and punch me in the back when I'm queuing for lunch."

"Who are these kids?"

"Just kids."

"Do they only pick on you or everyone?"

"Just me, I think."

"What do you do about it?"

"I tell Miss."

"Does she tell them off?"

"Not sure."

"Do you ever hit them back?"

"No, mum says it's naughty."

"Sometimes you've got to stick up for yourself or try to be their friend, maybe."

"Shall I give them sweets?"

"No, don't do that."

"Why not?"

"It doesn't work."

"Mum said I've to smile at people. Shall I do that?"

"Yeah, sometimes. And frown too. You know, if someone's making you mad."

"Like this?"

He pulled a face.

"No, don't do that. They'll laugh."

It's hard to tell a kid, especially a trusting, good-hearted kid such as Niall, how to be a 'man'—that it's a way of being, how

144

you stand and walk, hold yourself, speaking a certain way, sussing out a room, sitting with your back to the wall, holding eye contact for the right length of time. And that to earn respect you have to become adept at the balance of criticism and praise, enthusiasm and indifference. You also had to show you had a temper, not mind hitting out if it came to it or taking a punch.

My mind went back to James Lucas, a lad from my school. He didn't get it, the masculinity thing. He spoke as if he was a posh grown-up, routinely announcing that he was at 'the end of his tether' and constantly saying the word 'actually'. He was happiest among the girls or with a teacher, helping tidy the stock room or gluing sheets of paper on the inside jackets of books in the school library.

I heard the first inkling of the plot to get him while waiting in the corridor before a lesson. Three or four lads were sniggering. They had grown taller and bigger than the rest of us, flushed with unexpected power. James's mannerisms had been noted: the comic officiousness, the spiky self-confidence, the lightness of touch. He had it coming. We filed into the changing rooms for double Games. Mr Barton was in the gym preparing for circuit training; we could hear him positioning the benches. They cornered James. He was sitting beneath the clothes pegs, reluctantly fishing out the contents of his kit bag (he detested PE actually, he told everyone). They punched him a few times around the arms and pulled him to the ground. He began thrashing. Four or five lads were standing over him shouting encouragement to one another. The bodies and blur of movement made it difficult to see what was happening.

James was lifted from the ground. They had removed his top clothes. He was still kicking out. His trousers and boxer shorts were tugged roughly down beyond his knees. A cheer rose from the throng to celebrate his nakedness. The skin was bright white against the greys and blacks of school uniforms around him. He stopped writhing and fell still in their arms. As they made their way out, he was held aloft horizontally like a felled tree. They had planned a final indignity. The doors of the girls' changing room were booted open and he was hurled to the floor in front of them. He sprang to his feet and fled down the corridor, out on to the school field and ran for home, naked. We didn't see James for weeks afterwards. When he finally came back he was put in a different class.

I resolved to spare Jenny this story but it made me realise how important it was to get it right with Niall. Children *were* cruel.

Sunday, a week later

Loachy asked me to go to a rock concert with him. While I was there I could barely concentrate; my thoughts were louder than the music. It was the Sarah-Kate issue again. On the way home I decided finally to talk to him about my situation. He kept saying I was a dark horse and began hitting the centre of the steering wheel with the heel of his hand.

"You dark horse, you fucking dark horse. Why are you going with this Kate girl if you don't like her very much?"

"I do like her but I think I might have the capacity to like her too much, if you know what I mean."

"I'm not sure I do," he laughed.

I tried to explain. He nodded but I don't think he really understood. I was surprised he didn't ask more about her, show more interest—all that steering wheel banging and shrieking and yet not a single supplementary question. Didn't he recognise how monumental all this was, that my life might swing on an axis of either one woman or the other or none at all or both at the same time? It might even define me forever. I had to ask:

"Have you no more questions?"

"Not really, man. Should I have? It's late and I'm really tired."

Yes, you should. You should be teeming with them, wanting to pick through this morass of bubbling up emotions and moods and feelings. That's what friends did: listen, share, empathise, counsel. I thought, for a minute, of putting him right, really spelling it out: his selfishness, his insensitivity. I looked across. He was nodding his head in time to the music played on the CD player, mouthing the words.

I asked him to drop me off about half a mile from home, telling him I wanted a walk and would go via the park. I expected him to be surprised by this, perhaps a bit worried; it was now the early hours. He pulled to the kerb.

"There you go, mate."

In the moment, the walk felt to make perfect sense; I'm not sure why. It was strange going from a packed, noisy concert hall to an empty and dark outside place. The sky was empty of stars. The park was unlit and where the path cut through bushes, the blackness joined up on all sides. The smell was incredible, much more concentrated than usual, the daylight usual: at different places soily, grassy or floral.

I freewheeled down the banking to a stream where me and Niall had built a dam a year or so before. I threw in a stone to make sure the water was still there in the darkness. As my eyes grew accustomed I could see how the fallen leaves and twigs had merged with the peat beneath and made the water sludgy. The quietness was beautiful. I sat on a rock. I was hoping the setting—which I'd sought purposely to resemble a scene, *the* scene, in a film—might inspire a resolution: Sarah or Kate.

Mine and Sarah's lives were enmeshed. We talked. We worked. I was still attracted to her, impressed by her. I could find faults in her, in us, but wouldn't that be the case with anyone or any relationship after a handful of years. I had projected an affair on to her (with Ben) but it was unlikely, really; it was my unfounded fears played out rather than a consequence of her actions, her nature. She wasn't flirty. She wasn't particularly demonstrative with her affection but this didn't mean it wasn't there, merely well-managed.

Kate, in John's terms, *did* make your ears pop. I don't know how this happens with certain girls but every gesture and movement (of the eyes, mouth, lips, crossing of the legs, leaning forward to pick up a glass, talking, smiling, walking) had a sexual undertone. At first I'd wondered whether this magnetism was perceptible only to me but then I noticed other men staring, transfixed. They all wanted to take her home. She wasn't the type of girl with whom to fall in love, though; you sensed that hurt and trouble lay ahead. She was someone who knew too well the pervasive nature of men, what they were thinking and how to out-scheme them. I knew this because it had drawn me in, caught me out. So, the moment before you fell for her would be the last time you'd hold any power. After that, you were hers. She would toy with others (though pass it off as exuberance, a lust for life and nothing more) and, later, 'forget' to phone or text you. When she said she'd be having a few drinks with pals after work, you'd still be waiting, hoping, ticking off time, pacing the floor at seven o'clock going on to midnight, going on to tomorrow. What had she been up to? How far had you slipped from her thoughts? Should you, on her return, be confrontational or conciliatory? Should you swallow down more of your real feelings for fear of appearing the zealous and jealous boyfriend? How was the rest of your life to be played out—breathe deeply and often and give her the room to be, or remain coiled, on edge, stalked by the fear of her moving on, moving out? Her lips and her kiss were intoxicating but imagine being on your tiptoes always, trying to stand as tall as her charisma, her appeal. At quieter times—tea and toast in a rainy day café or you and her and a bottle of wine in a cosy cottage—she might promise a forever together but a woman who liked men so much, who knew them so well, was quicksand.

I soon began to feel cold. Damp was soaking into my clothes and bones. The splendour of the solitude had disappeared, spirited away by the chill-breeze through the trees. I found the path and headed home, walking briskly. I had to finish with Kate.

*

Jenny continued to push. It had become a fixation, discovering as much as possible about what was wrong with Niall. He had developed a persistent cough and complained of tightness around his chest. He was given two inhalers, one grey, the other brown. Eventually she was granted an appointment with the main paediatric consultant, Mr Mahmood.

Dad couldn't understand why Jenny was so determined.

"He's got anaemia, hasn't he? So what if it's a fancy version?" he said. "Why do you want them poking about with him? It's going to make the lad paranoid."

"You can't be in the dark over these things, merely hoping for the best," she said. "You've got to be able to make informed decisions."

"Informed decisions. I keep hearing that all the bloody time. Just trust people to do their job and to know what they're doing."

Monday

As I entered his study Joe carried on exactly where he'd left off a few days earlier.

"Do I sound a bitter man to you—all that wailing the other day?" he asked.

"I'm not sure."

"I probably *am* bitter but I'm not sure we ever see it in ourselves. At least, not clearly. It's a big admission, isn't it, bitterness? Or to give it another name—failure. We can busy ourselves, of course, hoping the white noise of our industry drowns out the reality but it's always there, building up as you get older. I know for a fact that I won't be published again, not properly anyway. Some half-arsed, piss-poor local outfit might take a punt but how will that compare to what I've had before? Back in the day, I don't think any book published ever sold fewer than, I don't know, 20,000 copies."

I noticed how much he was filling the chair, thinking how I'd hate to be that big. You could never slip by, go undetected. Wherever you went, on a bus, walking down the street, you were always this great slab of flesh. I wondered how much this had formed his character. You couldn't be timid or diffident in that frame, it would look like forced understatement. He carried on:

"Anyhows, Boo Boo, what I'm coming to is how all this affects me, and you. All of us, in fact. Do we—the lecturers, the university, the institution—carry on regardless and keep churning you lot out? That's what the old fraud Sinclair would like. As long as we're meeting targets, thus receiving our funding, he doesn't give a shit about the aesthetics of education, how we're supposed to nourish and develop minds. No, nothing as fancy as that, kiddo, but ever onwards in priming people for an industry that is basically fucked."

He stopped talking for a few seconds, looking up at the print of the Caves of Drach.

"Do you know what's needed? Bravery, that's what. They should all wise up to that Chinese proverb: better one day a tiger than a thousand years a sheep. We need writers brave enough to write what they want. Editors bold enough to publish what they'd really like to. We're at crisis point and it pisses me off that we ignore it at this university. We're all on a cloud, the staff I mean, floating above it all, acting as if everything is super and clinging to this notion of literary purity and self-determination, playing up to Sinclair's ideal. Well, it's not a fair world out there. It's corrupt, driven by greed and short-termism and it's making a mockery of us."

"What about the internet?" I asked.

"What about it?"

"It gives us access to every library in the world. You could argue that knowledge and literature has never been so easily available. Words on a screen are of no less value than on a page."

"I've been hearing that for years. It's all bite-size, no time for detail or reflection. We're reading cereal packets when we should be reading books."

He locked his fingers together, turned his hands round and pressed against the joints causing them to crack. I winced.

"Sorry, an old habit. Hey, don't look so glum."

How else was I supposed to look? He'd more or less told me that everything about the course, everything about me and my future, was futile.

They did two more days of tests on Niall, similar to what they'd done before but in greater detail. On the first day mum went with Jenny to the hospital and said they were in and out of examination rooms, fixing him up to machines, making him drink coloured fluid, giving blood, asking him questions. At the end of the second day they had a meeting with the consultant. I went too — Jenny insisted because 'I never forget a thing' and might be needed afterwards to prompt her memory.

"The results of these tests give me no cause for alarm," said Mr Mahmood.

The aplastic anaemia appeared to be under control and responding satisfactorily to medication.

"I am not going to suggest any treatment further to that he is already having," he said.

"Where does this leave us then?" asked Jenny.

Here it came, his great tablet of wisdom, all those years of study and experience, research papers piled high, bookcases crammed with learned tomes, mini digital recorder on the desk and countryside calendar on the wall:

"I am sure he will grow out of it."

Sunday, a week later

I went back to the same bar with Kate. The man who'd congratulated me on my good fortune of being her boyfriend wasn't there. The place was almost empty, in fact.

"I really like you," I told her. "But I can't go through with this."

"I thought not," she said.

"I guess I'm pretty old-fashioned when it comes down to it." ('I guess?'— I'd never said that before.)

She looked away.

"Are you okay?" I asked.

"Not really."

"I'm sorry."

She was filling up. I held her hand.

"I didn't mean to mess you about like this."

"Bit late for that now."

I fiddled with a beer mat on the table. Tap, tap. She asked me what I meant by old-fashioned.

"You know, a one-woman man, I suppose."

"You have a high regard of yourself, don't you?"

"How do you mean?"

(I was trying to stay cool now. Scratching at the mat. Wishing myself away, past the fluorescent posters advertising tapas nights and 'acoustic performers').

"With your course and everything, where you're encouraged to express yourself all the time. Just because you can write, it down doesn't mean you feel it any more than anyone else."

I was going to protest but she carried on.

"I don't think you've ever really considered me, my feelings."

She stopped and I filled the space by saying the worst thing possible. It would have been better to put up a counterargument rather than issue fake civility.

"I understand why you might feel like this."

She shook her head.

I took a drink of my beer and swilled it around my mouth. My throat was tense. I looked at the drink in her hand. I wondered—though I had no grounds to expect this, for she seemed calm—whether it was coming my way if I didn't watch out, straight in the face.

"I'm going," she said.

"Let me give you a lift."

"I'll find my own way home, thank you very much."

"No, come on," I pleaded.

She got in the car. She was crying. I said I was sorry again and asked if it was okay if I stayed in touch, as a friend.

"We've never been friends. You've not given us chance to be."

"I thought I had."

"If you did you've got a funny idea of what friendship is. You know hardly anything about me."

"I do. You've got a mum who's agoraphobic, a dad who died of a heart attack after an industrial injury." [I was blurting this out, made nervous by the situation, babbling.]

"Please be quiet. Do you think I want to be remembering my dad at a time like this? Please get me home."

When we got to the house she climbed out of the car in silence. I thought she'd slam the door but she shut it carefully, tripping across the pavement and through the front door. I drove off. When I was a mile or so down the road, the phone sounded. It was her. I parked up.

"Do you know what it's like to fall in love with someone and them not feel the same way?" she said.

She went quiet. Suddenly:

"Why don't you like me, anyway?"

"I do like you. I like you a lot but I'm going out with someone else."

"Why her and not me? What does she have that I don't?"

"It's not like that."

"What is it like?"

"It's whenever you meet people, really, where you're at."

"You're talking mumbo jumbo."

"It's the chronology, everything in life is. If I'd have met you before I met Sarah I'd be with you now. But I didn't and we've established a relationship, me and Sarah, got settled."

"Well, why did you start seeing me at the same time, then?"

"I wanted to see what would happen."

"Well, surprise surprise, someone ended up with a broken heart."

"Kate, you always knew I was with someone else."

"Are you telling me in a roundabout way that I should have kept the brakes on, made sure my feelings were kept in check?"

I think I probably was but to confirm this would have been patronising. In truth, I did think it odd that she could fall so deeply in love after a series of nights out and weekly bouts—the word feels appropriate for our encounters—of sex. We'd not spent tracts of time together; had day trips out and she hadn't met any of my friends or family. Nor me, hers. What was the basis of her commitment, then, and such hurt? I didn't know whether to be flattered that I could have this effect or pity her for placing such importance on a relatively paltry life-exchange. I was immediately disappointed with myself for having these thoughts. Wasn't she to be admired for giving herself, for trusting? I'd undertaken a mission of delusion every time I'd seen her, promising so much with my interest in her, my flattery, my expressing dissatisfaction over my relationship with Sarah. She had listened so attentively, offered support and understanding, not once judging or criticising Sarah or questioning why I was involved with someone who I often felt was disrespectful to me, moody, and whom I sometimes doubted even held me any real affection. Kate, in her own way, had, I saw now, been working away to make me believe it wouldn't be like that with her and now I was rejecting this offer, returning to, as she saw it, a love substandard.

Still, I'd made my decision, delivered it, and the best I could do was at least show that I cared for her feelings.

"Kate, please listen."

"I'm listening."

"I am so, so, very sorry."

I heard her sobbing.

"Please don't cry."

Strange, during the exchange in the pub and then on the phone, I became aware of an unimagined side to Kate. She was so busy being real and true that all that sex stuff fell away. She was almost like a child in her directness. I expected to feel relief at this point, the job finally done, but I wondered if I was letting someone special slip through my fingers. The sex siren persona was clearly an act, cover for someone more usually considerate and sweet. Even now, she wasn't responding with spite. She was perplexed and wounded but her instinct wasn't to strike out and tear down. After the phone call I drove around, crisscrossing the streets and out into the surrounding countryside.

It was nearly 3am when I arrived home. I could see movement through the frosted glass in the front door. I went inside. Niall was on the settee wrapped in a blanket. Mum and Jenny were tending to him, asking whether he had enough water and did he still feel poorly.

"What's wrong?"

"We've had the doctor out. She thinks he's got chickenpox. He's covered in spots, the poor thing."

I stood over him. He was curled up, eyes half-closed.

"How you doing, Mr Niall?"

"I'm all shivery," he said.

Jenny was at my shoulder.

"He keeps saying that but his temperature is sky-high."

"You'll soon be all right, Nially, I promise."

While I crouched at his side mum said:

"Sarah rang for you earlier. She said she couldn't get you on your mobile. I thought that's who you'd gone out with."

"No, I was with Loachy," I lied.

"Well you'd better call her first thing in the morning. She sounded fed up."

Monday

I rang Sarah while I was driving back to university. She was unusually abrupt:

"Where were you last night? I kept phoning."

"You should have texted."

"I thought I'd get through eventually but you were engaged for ages."

"The phone must be playing up. I'll get it checked."

There was a short silence before she asked:

"Will you be coming home during the week?"

"I didn't plan to but something's happened with Niall, so I might now."

I knew the gravitas of this statement would allow me to move the conversation from its earlier course.

"What's happened?"

"He's gone down with something. They think it might be chickenpox."

"Is it related to his anaemia thing?"

"We're not sure yet. They had the emergency doctor out last night but he's seeing his normal GP this morning."

I'd barely come to a halt on the university car park when Birtles scurried over.

"Heard the news?"

"No, what?"

"Joe's been suspended."

"How come?"

"Lots of rumours are flying around. He's supposed to have lost it and chinned Sinclair."

"Really?"

"Either that or he's touched up a first-year History student, one or the other."

"They're wildly differing incidents, Adam."

"I know, that's what I thought."

He swallowed hard, blinked and repositioned the Shredded Wheat.

During the morning I received a text message from a number I didn't recognise: 'Expect a grilling from Sinclair. Please don't say a thing. Joe' Almost as soon as I'd finished reading it,

Andrew, who had been giving the lecture, told me I had to see Sinclair immediately.

I knocked on the door of the administration department and was led to Sinclair's office, a small room off the main section. He had framed photographs of what I assumed were his grandchildren propped on a metal cabinet and, above them, fastened to the wall, a caricature of him playing golf, swinging wildly at the ball, his face felt-tip red.

"Please sit down," he said, pointing to the chair in front of him.

He was bald but unlike Loachy didn't shave his head, so had a band of grey hair stretching from ear to ear. He smiled. After what Joe had said about him I expected a lizard's tongue to protrude from his lips.

"I'm sorry we've not met before," he said. "Are you enjoying your course?"

"Yeah, it's good."

"Just good?"

He seemed genuinely interested. I was suspicious, wondering if this was technique, softening me up. He was extremely thin and, despite the grey hair, had the mien of a relatively young man. I had never really thought of Joe's age but assumed he was a generation or so younger than Sinclair. Now, across the table from him, I saw that they were both probably of a similar age.

"Do you know why I've asked to see you today?"

Here we go.

"Is it about Joe?"

He nodded and looked at me over his glasses.

"Over the next few days I'm hoping to speak to all the students who form his tutorial group. I've been chatting with Adam Birtles and he tells me you're quite close to Joe. Is this right?"

"I've had a few appraisals with him," I said. "What's he supposed to have done?"

"I'm afraid it's not 'supposed', it's what he *has* done."

His expression changed. He became more serious.

"What form did these appraisals take?"

"I'm not altogether sure what their purpose is," I said. "He's been talking about literature and the publishing world. Normal stuff really, I suppose."

"You wouldn't say he brought up anything inappropriate?"

I looked around the room as an indicator that I was taking the question seriously, raking through my memory.

"No, nothing."

Sinclair said he had to carry out more investigations and might want to speak to me at a later date. He thanked me and, as I turned to leave, shook my hand and said he hoped I'd continue to enjoy my time at university.

In Joe's absence most lectures were cancelled and it became an unofficial reading week; this allowed more time for rumours to spread. The most common—and it grew stronger day by day—was that he'd been 'grooming' a first-year student (no one was sure of the gender) and when confronted by Sinclair had lost his temper, pinning him against a wall.

"Do you think he'll get the sack?" I asked Lana Goldsmith while we waited to be served in the refectory.

"Long overdue."

"Being weirdy faggy is all well and good and perfectly legal," said her sister, Esther. "But grooming is a definite, total no-no."

"What *is* grooming?" I asked.

I knew what the word had come to mean and thought the girls would realise this and understand I was seeking a greater definition.

"Everyone knows what grooming is," chastised Esther.

"But when is it grooming and not just talking, being genuinely interested in someone? It doesn't have to be because you want to have sex with them."

Cardigan Barry, standing a few places behind us in the queue, interjected (unconcerned that several people we didn't know were overhearing):

"Or it might start out as talking and a sexual relationship develop naturally. You could argue that any courtship or virtually any personal interaction stands to be viewed as grooming."

"I never thought I'd hear you speaking up for Joe," I said.

He winced.

"I'm making a technical point. Another thing, if this girl or boy is at university won't he or she be at least eighteen? Should we be calling it grooming when it's someone beyond the age of consent?"

"It might be someone's younger sister or brother who was visiting for the weekend, something like that," said Esther.

"We all know what Joe's like, how manipulative and creepy he is," added Lana.

"I'm afraid that wouldn't be admissible in court. In fact, it would be sub judice to even hint that someone might be of such a character," said Barry.

Unusually, Sarah was working late most nights through the week and unable to make the routine six o'clock phone calls. I told her it was okay, not to worry. I was enjoying the space between us and the anticipation of seeing her again. I thought occasionally of phoning or texting Kate, if only to show I wasn't so heartless as to put her immediately and easily out of mind.

I called Jenny a couple of times and she told me Niall was recovering from his bout of chickenpox. His temperature had fallen and the spots were fading. She asked me again to have that talk with him about 'how to be a man' and to try and save him from being bullied.

Friday

I travelled home in the evening and, the next morning, took Niall to the hippy café above the wholefood shop in the town centre; his school was closed for a teacher training day. I liked the food at the café: the pulses, the nuts, the pastas, the salads and the homity pie. Niall liked it too and, whenever we went, I felt as if it was doing him extra good, filling him up with chewy and healthy stuff.

We climbed the stairs slowly, moving at Niall's pace. When we reached the top there was a woman sitting on a couch.

She was wearing a woollen hat with a flap that fastened under the chin, tight nylon tracksuit bottoms, fingerless gloves and a jacket with a print of giraffes on the shoulder patches. Behind her was a notice board teeming with handwritten cards offering aromatherapy, rooms to let, massages, camper vans, private music lessons ('not stuffy!!!'), lifts to work and acupuncture.

Most of the food was on plates in a large glass case. As usual, Niall took ages picking what he wanted. He walked along, laughing and barking orders:

"That. No, not that. Behind it. Yeah, that. No. What's that? That pasta thing, there. Has it got apples in it? Is it a pudding, do you think?"

I ordered him a pasta salad and a pie made from lentils and mushrooms. We sat by the window overlooking the road. He was still a bit lethargic after the chickenpox but a lot better, with only a handful of spots remaining ("Have me chicking pots gone yet?" he'd asked me in the car). Jenny said he'd been sleepy most afternoons and I noticed his eyes were heavy when he climbed on to his seat in the cafe, reaching across to dip his finger into my latte. He wanted the froth from the top.

"Can I have some frost?" he said, tilting his head cheekily. This was my chance for our 'chat'.

I asked if any kids had been punching or kicking him at school.

"I don't think so." he said.

"If they do, stick up for yourself, won't you?"

He nodded.

"Sometimes you've got to hit people back or shout at them."

I could tell he wasn't listening properly.

"I'm boring," he said.

He still hadn't learned the difference between the words boring and bored; he was telling me he was bored.

"I'm just boring," he said.

Across the room the giraffe print woman had been joined by two friends: a drippy looking bloke wearing a tatty combat jacket, and a woman in black jeans, black coat and black-dyed dreadlocks. She had a toddler with her called Joey; all three kept saying his name. They were very tactile with him and between all the touching and stroking they asked if Joey was all right, what Joey wanted to eat, what fun it was that Joey was knocking into chairs and charging about (they didn't seem to mind him being reckless). He must have wanted something particular to eat because they sent him to the counter to ask for it himself. They were very pleased that he completed this mission and cheered him back to the table, helping him on to a chair and forming a huddle. After a second or two they threw their arms in the air and began cheering. Joey had said something so funny and incredible that they laughed and clapped for ages. The bloke even stamped his feet.

Joey then wandered over to the window, pointing at the passing cars and lorries, trying to engage Niall who was smiling at him from about three metres away. I saw Joey's mum's eyes fall sly and she clawed at the air. She was immediately on her feet, scowling, pointing.

"Has he got chickenpox?" she demanded.

I didn't have time to answer.

"What are those spots on his face?"

She grabbed at her son, pulling him roughly away. He was

bewildered and started crying. She had to shout above the bawling.

"Fancy bringing him out when he's got chickenpox," she screamed.

I looked at Niall's face. Three or four spots were around his forehead but they were shrunk and spent. I was surprised she'd even seen them from the other side of the café and also that she'd guessed what they were: didn't kids often have spots and blemishes on their faces? Before the intrusion, I'd been happy in that special warmth and satisfaction that comes when you're in close and loving proximity to a child. I wasn't prepared for an argument and said something stupid.

"What am I supposed to do with him?"

She was back sitting at her table, clutching Joey to her side. I was angry, angrier than I'd ever been before in a public place. I was beyond words and wanted to turn over their table, smash their plates to the floor. I was compromised by Niall; I didn't want him to see me lose my temper. They must have seen the madness in my face because all three fell silent, looking down at the table, the dreadlock woman still shaking her head.

Outside, on the way back to the car, I was frustrated that I'd not said and done something. I tried to defuse my rage by talking to Niall.

"That lady was naughty wasn't she, Niall?"

"Yeh."

"Why?"

He wasn't sure. He screwed up his face as if he was thinking hard.

"She smacked that Joey."

"No she didn't. She was shouting, wasn't she?"

"Yeah, that's it: shouting."

I didn't routinely phone people to relate specific incidents from my life but decided, with the zeal of someone discovering a new concept, that I'd call Sarah and tell her. That was what girlfriends were for, surely. She answered immediately:

"You'll never guess what's just happened..." I began.

"What?"

The downbeat tone of her voice reflected neither the unusualness of my phoning unexpectedly nor my beginning a conversation in such a peculiar way. It also suggested that she had little interest in guessing what had, in fact, just happened. I told her the story but felt as if she were hurrying me along. I wondered if she was compromised, being at work with colleagues overhearing.

"I'm on my lunch hour," she said, scotching that theory.

"Are you around tonight?" I asked.

"I think so," she said.

Think so? She'd not seen me for almost a week. What was all this about? I had a second to get my stab in first and emerge the victor.

"Damn, I've remembered. I said I'd see Al tonight," I said.

"Okay."

Okay? That's all? Since when had she adopted my games—this feigned indifference, the insouciance. This was going to incur a mountain of man-cruelty.

*

167

I dropped Niall off at Jenny's and as I got back into the car, the phone sounded.

"It's me," said Sarah.

"Hello."

"Do you think you could put off seeing Al tonight?"

I knew immediately, just knew. It was in her voice, the words spoken as if read from a card. She was going to finish me.

"Of course," I answered, feeling nauseous, my heart a sledgehammer. I don't know how I managed to form what I said next:

"Has something come up?"

"Sort of. I'll tell you later."

I put the phone on the seat next to me. I closed my eyes and slumped so that my forehead pressed against the centre of the steering wheel. The phone rang again and I sat upright, startled. It was Joe.

"Can I see you?" he asked.

I told him I had something planned. He was adamant.

"It's utterly and monumentally important," he said. "Are you on site?"

For a second I didn't understand what he meant.

"At the university?" he explained.

"No, I'm at home, about two hours away from uni."

"Let me have the address. I'll leave now."

I figured I could see him before meeting up with Sarah, if he set off immediately.

We met at a rundown pub on the outskirts of the town centre. I arrived first and he entered soon afterwards, looking about him furtively.

"Want a drink?" he asked.

"I'm sorted," I said, nodding towards the glass on the table.

As he stood at the bar, shifting his weight from foot to foot, I realised that although he was wearing similar clothes to those few others dotted around the pub, you could tell he wasn't one of them; it was something about how he carried himself. When he was passed the change for his drink I heard him say, 'fantastic' and there seemed a slight note of sarcasm as the barmaid responded: 'Anytime, love.'

He sat across from me. He said he had been 'having a dip' on the drive over. I asked what he meant. He took a hip flask from his pocket and waved it at me.

"Vodka, man. Hot and sweet."

He leaned forward, making the point that he was scrutinising me.

"What's up, man, you look glummed up," he said.

"I think I'm about to get dumped," I said.

"Fucking hell."

I told him about the meeting I was to have later with Sarah, how I was sure she was about to end the relationship. He held up the palm of his hand and nodded his head as if beseeching me to fall quiet.

"Some advice," he said. "If she says she wants to spend more time on her own or she wants some space or she feels she's settled down too young or wants a break to 'find herself' it all means the same thing."

"What's that?"

"She's met somebody else. They always leave you for

somebody else, always."

I told him we had been pretty happy together, most of the time.

"That doesn't matter," he said. "Women are fickle. They never know what they want. They're always looking for something else, something more. Imagine it like this—there's her, your girlfriend, and then there's an evil invisible twin sister trailing her. They're having a constant dialogue and the evil twin that never lived, which has made her extra bitter, is making her restless, telling her there is this and that to be had a little bit over the hill, slightly out of reach. When you're with her, your girlfriend, any girlfriend in fact, it's like sitting in a darkened room while this demon girl presses the trousers for your funeral. It's no wonder their heads are a mess, is it? They don't know real in-the-moment happiness, never will."

He was scaring me a bit; I'm not sure I understood the evil twin sister story. There was a slight pause before he started again:

"Any idea who the bloke is?"

"If there is one..."

"I've just told you—there will be one. It's the law."

"In that case it's probably someone from work."

"How imaginative. Love thy neighbour. Or the runt at the next desk inputting the same brain-dead data as you, all bloody day long. Right, I'll tell you straight and share the wisdom: this is how it will work. The first thing that'll get into your head, and this is natural so accept it, is that he is an infinitely greater sexual being than you. This is a male thing. I'm sure when you made love to her you did it with a good and honest heart, tried your best, but you were probably happy enough in the intimacy, almost indifferent to the performance. He, meanwhile—in your head at least, your imagination,—is standing in the doorway between the bathroom and the bedroom in the hotel where they're staying or a mate's flat they've borrowed for the afternoon. They're not splashing around playfully in the shallow waters of their sexuality. No, they mean business. Their pleasure will be athletic, sinewy, industrial and hardcore. Sometimes, you'll find yourself aroused by this image and your self-disgust and sadness will make you feel ill. When they've done with their sex, and this will take some time, he'll fall gentle and tender in the bedclothes. He'll smile and laugh, working at being all those things she told him you weren't, such as, for starters, attentive, relaxed and funny. You see, you never listened, pal, never cared. And, bless him, he might be thinking deep down that she's a little bit needy and wondering what she might say about him one day. But not today, hey? Today is for sexing it up, telling her anything she wants, being anything she wants."

I looked about me. Keep it quiet, will you? People round here don't talk like this. And that stuff about athletic and sinewy blokes—pure Nevile Thompson territory. Joe was smiling, showing far too many yellowing teeth.

"New lovers aren't like this really," he said. "Something happened in your past that makes you believe this shit. It's as if all your insecurities are writ large on the tallest, widest wall in your home town. Back when you didn't know to be prudent or wary, the hem of your real self got caught beneath someone's feet. You were mocked, shrunk to half your size and you stayed that way. Now you're back there, a boy-squeak of a man, thinking that even if you gave your best shot to this bloke stealing your woman, he'd take hold of your fist as if it was a fluttering butterfly and squeeze it to mush and dust. All your cleverness and cunning and college doesn't mean a thing here, son. All that's an untruth, my friend, believe me. Let's have it right, come on. Most likely, your usurper will be a pug-ugly, boring arsehole but the difference is that he's new and you're old. Once you're no longer a mystery to a woman they start getting bored. It's all to do with *them*. They want to feel new and lovely and excited, reborn to a new version of themselves, so they get a different bloke, start again. Think of the wondrousness of it all—new people to meet, places to go. It all leads back to the same place though—themselves, what they are, what they will always be, but it's a pleasant excursion, isn't it, and who cares if the poor bloke is a fucking broken biscuit afterwards, never quite the same. They don't see the mess. In fact, and you watch out that I'm right here, they usually disengage themselves completely from the circle of friends they mixed in when they were with you. That's how keen they are to start afresh and how little you and your mates and anyone associated with you mattered."

I breathed out extravagantly.

"Have you ever been accused of being a misogynist?" I asked.

"Fuck," he said. "That's one of those fire-words they use to torch any argument that's getting too near the truth, same as calling someone a racist if they dare utter anything outside the standard liberal orthodoxy. Fuck all that. Say it like it is."

"How come you know all this stuff?" I asked. A foolish question really; it was obviously drawn from personal experience.

"My wife, Helen, left me." His voice had softened slightly. "Are you ready for the pain?"

"I'm not sure," I said.

"You're going to feel shit for a very long time, my friend. You can try and hurry yourself away from it by travelling around, visiting people, drinking excessively, having sex with different people, working hard—in your case doing lots of writing, hopefully. But all this has little effect. The sadness, this peculiarly restless, screwed up version, travels with you like a rucksack full of sick. It'll be there on the plane to Greece or Thailand when you're trying your best to be someone else, someone not in pain, when you're heading to the sun and away from those runty wet streets you've walked all your life. It's there when you're talking passionately about something you care about among people that suddenly seem much more than friends and collectively form a new kind of 'love'. This is you filling a vacuum, nothing more. It's there in your headache hangover when you've read *The Lost Weekend* and wish more than anything that you could be a bona fide, out-of-it alcoholic to make life one beautiful, painless, pointless blur. It's especially there when you're on the easy sex vibe in a strange house surrounded by family photographs that you don't recognise and you're pulling roughly at someone's clothes, kissing them hard enough to hurt and imagining yourself as this non-caring, non-loving, all-physical ascetic porn star. And, of course, you can expect the circumstances of your breakup to ricochet forever around your head. You'll be driven, looking for clues to solve a crime that feels like murder. Every detail will be analysed and a searchlight taken to long-ago gestures and comments that had once seemed insignificant but may now resonate with a new significance. Take me, for example. Helen wrote me a letter when she left and in it she said that I had become unmysterious. I became obsessed with this fucking word. You become 'unmysterious' when you've given your all, held nothing back, and the very process of disarming mystery has bound you closer together. It is the definition of love, the love that supersedes romantic and passionate love. It is the love that you come home to, bathe in, wear like old clothes. While it's possible to change most things and at least try to make yourself lovable again, you cannot resuscitate mystery. It is the part that is sacrificed to give life to the greater whole. If someone grieves for the old version of you, the excitement of the unknown, it's time to leave. They have wrung you out, had enough. It's nothing personal. They want newness and you, however you dress it up, are old news; a spent conviction. So, back to my theme: if you can't find what you need by picking through the relationship, and this process alone will take months, you'll start thinking about your past, your partner's past, previous affairs, your family, your childhood. You'll be convinced that among all this is the flawed fuck up gene that caused you to be chucked up from life with all this time, miles and miles of it, days and days, stretching out before you like sludge. But, I tell you, all this thinking is futile. There was no murder. Your life was no different than anyone else's. You didn't do anything wrong and if you did you're kind of lucky because you know you deserve what you're now getting and this will help relieve the pain, a portion of it at least. And you're not on your own. Shit happens to everyone. All around: people on the train travelling to work, in the car next to you on the dual carriageway, walking down the street, probably even in this fucking pub. They might seem in control, cool and saintly in their togetherness, but a good number are taking their turn and dealing with it—illness, bereavement, sexual infidelity, crime. They don't carry placards or daub their condition on their cars in spray paint. They get on with it. Now it's your turn to walk among them and with appropriate nobility. Fake it if you need to, almost everyone else does. Fake it until you don't know you're faking it any more and it becomes your truth: whatever gets you through. You're not actually medically ill and you're not actually, really going to die, no matter how painful it feels. So you mustn't feel special in your suffering."

All those words, all those theories and statements. And hardly a breath. I had a disconcerting thought: what if I had misjudged Sarah's tone and she wasn't going to finish me. Perhaps she was to suggest we marry or we go out more or that we should live together. It would seem a shame that Joe's fantastical sermon had been unnecessary. He was slowly revolving his near-empty pint glass on the table. He began talking again.

"When Helen first went I embarked upon all the things I now tell friends not to. I literally cried to the sky. The day after her announcement I drove to the countryside and parked at the bottom of a steep hill. I was young then, in my late-twenties, and I ran hard, falling down exhausted. I finally picked myself up and walked until I came to a narrow path running along the edge of a precipice. At the bottom I could see the skull of a sheep surrounded by tufts of wool. A dog or fox had attacked it. I started thinking all this fanciful stuff about death and loneliness and imagined launching myself to the rocks. It began to rain and the wind picked up. It was June but felt like December. I liked the wildness; it suited my mood. My face was scorched by the cold and I shouted into the gale. I screamed at first and then yelled swear words. These profanities were blown back at me, sucked up by the wind and slapped across my face. Civilisation was a few hundred yards away but the environment was so hostile I felt as if I'd been ejected into outer space or out to sea, some place else. I wanted to stay there forever but after a while I began to shiver and I trudged back down the hillside."

"How did it affect you, being left?"

"I felt ill almost all the time. It was as if I'd swallowed a length of contaminated meat. In my mind's eye it was liver or something, saturated in blood and putrescent after being left out in the sun too long. It stretched from my throat to the bottom of my stomach, unable to pass either way. I expected this pain to manifest immediately and stared long into the mirror, incredulous that I wasn't covered in boils or my eyes staring out from jaundiced holes. At night, I thrashed around the itchy, empty double bed. When sleep finally came it was broken every few minutes as if it coexisted with an electrical charge that caused my body to convulse as soon as I relaxed. Some of Helen's clothes were still scattered around the bedroom—a black and yellow night-dress, the leggings she wore for her exercise workouts, tights wrinkled and folded like a concertina, shoes tipped on their side. I couldn't bring myself to pick them up and throw them away. Her hairs were everywhere. I had to fish them from the bath plughole where they'd set as a clump of sticky syrup. Within a month or so I deluded myself into believing that I was beginning to recover, building new routines, pushing the hurt further away but my emotions and my irritability were on a pilot light ready to flare up. I was fine as long as I slipped through the world unnoticed but I was susceptible to the slightest tilt of circumstance. If the lady in the post office smiled at me I was elated but if she frowned I felt like death. A rainy day was a conspiracy. Something breaking down—I remember the telephone went on the blink—made me want to beat myself with it until my vision ran red. All I could do was wait. Do you know what it is like to wait, to be aware of almost every minute and hope and pray that it won't be as painful as the last?"

I shook my head. I was bewitched by his eloquence, astounded by the lucidity of his memory but also unsettled.

"You recall it well," I said.

"It was a big, big deal," he said. "In hindsight I'd probably put far too much into my relationship with Helen, trusted too much. I'd had a really weird childhood with hardly any tactile love around or emotion in general. My dad was very old school and my mum was sort of in awe of him, frightened even, and showing any compassion or love was viewed as a weakness. I put into my relationship with Helen everything that should have been played out in my family life. Of course, I had none of this clarity of thought back then, when she skittered off. I was

177

pretty much the original, stereotypical fuck up. I was desperate to get her back. I phoned her, wrote, asked her repeatedly to return. I hinted to her brother, who I didn't particularly like, that he should spy on her for me. I think he noticed my tears of gratitude when he agreed to 'keep an eye on her'. I wrote rank poetry and kept an overwrought diary in which the handwriting veered from olde English curlicues and dips to fervent, blotchy scribbles. I couldn't sleep. I called on friends and made them stay up late: talking, talking, boring. I'd not seen some of them for years and when they opened the door I could sense their disappointment: what do you want after all this time? I lost weight. I developed a tickly cough and the doctor put me on a variety of inhalers. I drank so much beer I could smell it on me permanently. I sobbed at my parents' house and it was sometimes so bad that my dad had to leave the room, disgusted. I bought new clothes and went to clubs and pubs in search of women. I needed to fill the space at my side. More than once, I walked the streets on a Sunday morning, an hour or so after dawn, reeking of smoke and beer, my mouth dry, my head aching. Every few steps I'd catch the scent of last night's woman about me, the one I'd fucked with the rage of someone with hours to live. There I was, bones and clothes."

"What got you through?"

"Do you need to ask? One thing and one thing only. I put everything into my writing. Thank God I had a publishing deal at the time. Every drop of pain was squeezed into those books, spread out among the various characters. That's why they may seem so bleak and without hope: that's how I felt. I wasn't going to falsify some happy clapping for anyone and, anyway, you were given the freedom in those days to express whatever the hell you wanted. I don't recall a single conversation with my editor about narrative arc or tone or what the characters were up to in any of my novels. They left you to it and kept their fucking noses out of what they had no business in."

"Can I ask you something?" I said.

"Fire away."

As he'd told me he'd once been married, I had to amend the question slightly from the original I'd planned.

"Are you bisexual?"

"What makes you ask that?" he asked, all coquettish.

The list was long: the effeminate mannerisms; his walk, which was more of a sashay; the Nevile Thompson book; the stuff the Goldsmith twins had told me; his attitude to women (which was similar to that of one or two gay people I knew but much more aggressive).

"Just wondered."

"Since you ask, I'm not, actually. As much as they rattle and rile me, I'm strictly for the ladies."

I must have had a look of incredulity.

"I can understand your confusion. A few minutes ago when I said I'd never had a quarrel with an editor—I was fibbing. I had one and one only. I wanted to call my third novel, *The Sodomisers*. They wouldn't have it, which I kind of knew anyway but I wanted to cause some agitation—it's what I lived for then, got off on. It's hard to imagine now when homosexuality is so cuddly and mainstream but it was once a real maverick stance, an out-there statement of the personal and the political. I was fascinated by the whole culture. I think, to be honest, I wanted to be gay but couldn't force it. The Nevile Thompson book was me taking on a role, sort of daring myself. A psychiatrist would say I was kicking back at my father. He loathed homosexuals. He never called them gay or queer, always homosexuals or homos. The whole issue would bring him out in a cold sweat. I remember him once pointing to a photograph in a newspaper of an AIDS victim, this wretched emaciated bloke on the brink of death, and scoffing: 'Serves him right.' Slightly in his defence, it was the early days of AIDs and amid a real climate of fear. I argued that the bloke hadn't asked to be gay and my dad snapped at me: 'You're not a bloody homo, are you?' I remember the look in his eyes, fierce and determined. It felt as if I'd have uttered the word 'yes' in answer to his question he would have disowned me on the spot, booted me out of the door."

Time was moving on.

"Did you want to talk about Sinclair?" I asked.

"Fucking hell, I almost forgot all about him."

"Yeah?"

"I'm proud that I can do that."

"What?"

"Live truly in the moment. It's a skill. I've not slept for days thinking about Sinclair and the university and all that shit and yet for the last fifteen minutes I've been back there, years ago, being dumped by Helen, banging on about this and that. There is hope for me, if I work at it. It's like Helen going—you've got to steel yourself, believe in recovery, getting over it, one minute at a time, sweet Jesus. This particular crisis can't go on forever. I have to sleep eventually. There has to be peace."

For the first time, I looked properly at his clothes. He was shabby as if he'd been wearing the same ones for days.

"Peace, that's what I ask for," he said. "To be away from all this. I've always been in a film, my own film, where I'm the star, of course. From being a kid. They focus on my eyes, the expressions I make. I fill up the screen. I always see the camera and play to it. Except a few weeks ago the reel ran out. I wasn't there any more. Do you know what I'm talking about?"

"I think so."

"After all this stuff with Sinclair and Rachel, it faded to black, gone."

"Rachel?"

"Rachel is the new Helen, another who will throw dirt upon me eventually. She has the most gorgeous mouth you'll ever see. The lips are as fleshy as overripe plums. When we lie down together it's almost too perfect. I think of that corny song from years ago, way before your time, the lyric: 'Sometimes when we touch, the honesty's too much'. Why would that get into my head? Why would it suddenly have so much meaning? It's because true love is so honest. It takes from you everything bad and false. You are, in that minute, born again. The only thing you can do, the only physical response, is to cry. I have cried hard with Rachel. I have dabbed my tears and put them to her lips and she has tasted them, asked for more. The age gap doesn't matter. What the fuck has that got to do with anything? Why do people see evil where there is beauty? And what if she is a student and I am her teacher? This has been a path to true and deep love since time began. The Greeks were at it, for pity's sake. It's normal. When Sinclair called me

181

into his office he made me out to be this predatory, depraved, lascivious creature, a beast disguised as a man. I knew nothing of which he spoke. I told him it was love and all the words I used were appropriate, playful, warm and decent. But he couldn't hear them. I didn't want to fall upon Rachel and tear her to bits. I wanted to hold her aloft, make her lovelier and treat her with gentleness and honour."

"What actually happened?"

He frowned.

"What always happens when you're not listened to, when someone accuses you of a crime you didn't commit and never would, when they paint upon you cunning and guile after you have been nothing but open and trusting. He turned day to night, warmth to cold. He sullied it, me and Rachel, and he had what was coming.

"What was that?"

"I told him that if he did not stop talking I would kill him. Actually, it wasn't so much kill him as remove him. I had an instinctive feeling that I had to tear him down. It had the desired effect because he shut up and asked me to leave his office."

I was beginning to wonder what my part was in all this, why he had travelled over to see me. He read my thoughts.

"I have a feeling that Sinclair is going to call you in again," he said. "A few of the students have been aware that we've had get-togethers in my study and once he hears about this he's going to imagine something untoward has been going on."

"What kind of untoward?"

"Bummery, probably. They're compiling a dossier of

degeneracy on me. I'm supposed to be hitting on every student that comes within twenty five yards of me, male or female. They're also claiming that I've been revealing college secrets—how many paper clips we order each year, the weight of the consignment of elastic bands that arrived last week, that kind of thing. You know how obsessed Sinclair is with trivia."

I didn't actually; I knew very little about Sinclair.

"I've not come here to ask you to lie for me," he said. "Or to make you say anything you don't want to say, but only to point out that everything I've ever said to you, whether in the lectures or in my study, was done to make you a better writer, that's all. I had no other agenda. Since I've been suspended, everyone is analysing me and seeing nothing but chicanery and negativity. It's a dreadful thing to be held up as all the things you're not."

I was surprised that he was so sensitive to criticism. This was his next theme.

"You might be a bit shocked by how I've responded but when you're in that final room, metaphorically, you become who you really are—when you're under threat as I am here, my whole integrity. Day to day I'm the flinty character you've always assumed me to be and I don't honestly give a fuck about most things. But this is me, the me that is really me, if that makes sense. And we each have a set of principles we hold, so to have them attacked and eroded is painful. That's why three sleeping tablets won't knock me out at night. It wouldn't be so bad if I could see Rachel but since the whole furore broke, she's left university to go back home to her parents in Devon. I want to see her but Sinclair won't set a date for the hearing, which means I have to stick around. I feel like a fucking zombie walking through a dead town, bits of me falling off."

Our glasses had long been empty. I could overhear a bloke at the bar talking about football; it seemed absurdly trivial compared to the depth of our subject matter. The fruit machine was whirring and, in the other room, I could hear the click of pool balls. Joe didn't see the barmaid approaching over his shoulder.

"Are these glasses done with?"

Joe didn't answer but looked ahead, not focusing on anything in particular.

"Yes," I told her.

I looked at my watch.

"Am I holding you up?" asked Joe.

I told him I was due to see Sarah soon at Kava, a bar across town.

"Let's have a quickie, then," he said.

I said it was my round but he sprang from his chair and was at the bar within seconds. Three pints of beer were put on the counter and what looked like a whisky. He knocked the short back in one go and returned to the table clutching the pints.

"Three?"

"One for me, one for you and one for later," he said.

I told him I wouldn't have enough time to drink mine.

"That's fine. I'll finish it off, no problem."

We drank in silence until he asked:

"All briefed then on the Sinclair front?"

"Yes, all briefed. It's easy when all I've got to do is tell the truth."

He knocked back his first pint in almost a single gulp. Licking his lips, he said:

"One last thing—we have a mole, you know, a grunty, cunty little mole."

"Really?"

"Can't you guess who?"

Before I could nominate someone he said:

"It's Birtles. He's been placed on the course purposely to keep an eye on me."

"Are you sure?"

"Surer than sure. All that crap about him working for a local paper and then deciding he wants to be a novelist. He can't fucking write. He's my Mr Parkis, hired by Sinclair to watch my every move."

"I wouldn't worry about Birtles," I said. "He's too much of a space cadet to concern anyone."

"What if he's pretending to be a space cadet and he's actually terribly efficient and has reams of information on me? It wouldn't surprise me if he has followed me here today. Has he been saying anything to you?"

I didn't want to fuel his suspicion by revealing that he'd asked me if he was a gay.

"No."

I was starting to feel lightheaded, the spaced-out, slightly drunk feeling you sometimes get when drinking during the day.

"I've got to go," I said.

"You have. You have to face the woman and her invisible evil twin and you've got to be strong and proud and sure of yourself."

I thought he might be about to pull out a sabre and bring it down hard on the table as a sign of our manly kinship.

"I'll do my best," I said, resisting the urge to salute.

Outside, the air smelled rich and fresh. People were making their way home from work, dashing to cars, queuing at bus stops. I texted Sarah that I was running a few minutes late. A message lit up almost instantaneously: 'No worries'. When I reached Kava I stalled for a second outside. This was, I was sure, the last time I would be part of this relationship: me and Sarah. In an hour or so I would exit this building alone, life changed. My fingers tingled with nerves and runnels of sweat formed at my armpits, trickling down my skin.

She was sitting in a raised part of the bar, an area surrounded by a short latticed fence. She waved and gave me a tight tense smile.

"Do you want a drink?" I asked, despite noticing that the glass in front of her was almost full.

"I'm fine, thanks."

I bought a drink and returned to the table.

"I've something to tell you," she said.

"Yeah?"

"I've met someone else."

So, she hadn't told me she wanted to spend more time on her own or that she wanted some space or felt that she had settled down too young or wanted to 'find herself'. I was getting the truth. No fudging the issue, no disingenuousness. She had met someone else.

"What about us?"

She said it had all gone—the magic, the oomph, the sparkle.

"We've become like brothers and sisters," she said. "It's no one's fault, it's just happened that way."

I watched her mouth as she talked. I felt to be with a stranger. It was as if she was speaking a foreign language. I gazed at the grain in the wood panel behind her, wishing I could look at it for the rest of my life. I told her it was easy to go off with someone else and everything would be exciting for the first few months but our relationship was special, something that had lasted and might come along only once in a lifetime.

"Doesn't it mean anything to you?" I asked.

"Yes, of course it does. It's confusing."

She looked for a second as if she was reconsidering. At this point, when it seemed hope was being regenerated, it was extinguished, stamped out. She spoke as if she was reading aloud a mantra, every word clearly pronounced.

"I know what we've had has been really special and everything and I know I probably won't meet anyone as good for me as you again and I might regret this for the rest of my life, but I've met someone I've never felt this way about before. It's as if I don't have any choice but to be with him."

I had to ask.

"Who is he?"

I knew she was going to say Ben, the bloke I'd seen her with after I'd been to the hospital. I watched her lips, waiting for this tiny, one-syllable word to form.

"Matthew," she said.

"Matthew?"

"You've probably heard me refer to him more as Mr King."

"Mr King? Mr King, your boss—he's in his thirties."

"Thirty eight, actually."

"Isn't he married?"

"Not for much longer."

"Kids?"

"Three—two girls, aged 11 and 12, and a baby boy."

"How old is the baby?"

"Six weeks."

"Jesus, Sarah, you're talking serious carnage there."

"It depends how you choose to view it."

"What other way is there?"

"It's stuff you've got to go through to get to where you want to be."

"What does his wife think of it all?"

"She doesn't know yet. He's not told her. It's a token marriage, anyway. She doesn't love him, not properly. She talks down to him all the time, treats him like a kid. She nags and nags at him, nothing's ever right. He deserves better. He's a good man."

It sounded as if she was going to be with him out of charity.

"*I'm* a good man" I said.

"I know you are."

"What's the difference, then?"

"It's how I feel. I can't change that."

"What about his kids, are you going to bring them up?"

"I'm assuming they'll stay with their mum, that's what usually happens. I can't worry about all that, though. I believe if their dad is happy, and he will be with me, they'll be happy and okay, too."

"That's a bit simplistic, isn't it?"

"Things are often more straightforward than you make out. You always put too much thought into everything."

"While we're here, is there anything else about me that you don't happen to like?"

"Don't go there."

"I want to learn."

"You don't really."

"I do."

"If that's the case then, I feel like you control me. It's the way you look at me, sort of disapproving. You put me on edge. Everything has to be how you want it. I can't stand that expression you pull when you're angry but trying your best to look as if you're not. And I don't think you've ever had any plans to properly commit yourself to me—girls like that, you know: marriage and everything."

"You've never said that before."

"Shouldn't need to, some things are obvious."

"I don't understand. If you think I control you and make you unhappy why, at the same time, are you pissed off that I've not asked to marry you?"

"Security and commitment are important."

"That doesn't answer the question."

"I don't have to answer just because you're trying to force me. It's not about outwitting each other or who wins an argument. It's about how things have gone, how we feel. Another girl might not see things like I do. She might see it differently and like what you are, everything about you. And that's the girl for you. Maybe *I* do things that annoy *you* and it brings out your worst side."

"Is anybody truly happy in their relationship? Isn't there always something wrong?" I asked.

"I don't know but I'm not giving up on the ideal. I'm too young. If I feel it, and I do with Matthew, I'm going to follow my heart."

"No matter what affect it has on other people?"

"You can't live your life like that. There are some things beyond explanation or logic and they just happen. And when they do, you have to follow. The alternative is to give up your life, the life you really want, and it's not fair on the other person, that."

"You mean me?"

"Yes, you. You deserve to be with someone who feels for you like I do about Matthew. It's what you're due."

"I thought you felt that way."

"I did and for a few years but now it's passed. Things change and you have to change with it, move on. When my dad died I had to work through a lot of stuff, decide what I was and what I wanted."

"I helped you through all that."

"To a point."

"What do you mean?"

"On the night of the funeral, when I needed you the most, you left me alone and went out with your mates. How do you think that made me feel?"

"But you said it was okay. I did it with your blessing."

"I might have said it was okay but it was a question you shouldn't even have been asking. I was so amazed and disgusted, I said yes for the sake of it. None of my friends could believe what you did."

I shook my head, incredulous.

"What does your mum think about what you're doing?"

"Don't bring my mum into it. That's not fair."

"I imagine that with her being religious and all that, she's not so keen on... [I stopped for a second, wondering whether I should actually say the word]...adultery."

"She's right behind me, if you must know, " she snapped. "She wants her daughter to be happy."

"What do we do now?" I asked.

"You go home or to Al's or Loachy's or wherever you're planning and I'm going to meet Matthew and tell him what's happened."

"Exactly the same as you did when you dumped Dan for me. Ever the efficient one, aren't you? It might not be so easy this time, though, with a wife and kids involved, not to mention all the various other family members who will be devastated."

"Don't talk like that."

"Don't talk the truth?"

"No, stop trying to bully me. It makes me even more sure that what I'm doing is the right thing. People who love one another, or say they do, don't talk like you're talking now. They show concern and support and then move on."

"Even when they're all cut up inside?"

She fell quiet before proffering: "Yes."

"Well I'm sorry I failed the test."

My fist was clenched. Sarah noticed.

"You're not going to do anything stupid, are you?" she asked.

"What like?"

"I don't know, make a scene or something and start threatening Matthew. I like to think you're above all that soap opera stuff. There's no good guys or bad guys when this happens. It's horrible and sad for everyone."

"Not for you it isn't."

"It is. I've been tortured. I've not slept for weeks. I can't eat. Haven't you noticed how much weight I've lost? I don't know how I'm coming across now but this isn't easy, you know. I do have feelings for you, strong feelings. You can't be with someone over a period of time and not do. I knew you wouldn't be able to accept this like most people."

"What does that mean?"

"You go so much into everything, all the ins and outs."

"I'm sorry about that. I thought you liked that side of me. You used to tell me you enjoyed all that sharing of feelings, being open with you."

"I did."

"What happened, then?"

"I suppose it's one of the things that changed. Like I said, it just happens."

"Does Matthew share his feelings?"

"Not like you do."

"What's that supposed to mean?"

"You're trying to outsmart me again, aren't you? You want me to compare Matthew to you, to draw him into the same ring, measure it all out. He's different than you and I like different things about him, let's leave it there."

I suddenly remembered a few things about him.

"Didn't he used to tell you all he'd been a professional

footballer but you found out that he was lying? And doesn't he play golf?"

"So what, if he plays golf?"

"My God, Sarah, you're leaving me for an old bloke who plays fucking golf. You're going to get fed up with him in three months. And those kids will be dragging you all over the place."

I became aware of movement to my left. It was a large man carrying a coat, about to sit down at an adjacent table. It was Joe. He had a black eye. I was about to ask him what had happened when he started up.

"What is she telling you? What has the evil twin put her up to?"

I wondered if it might be possible to pass him off to Sarah as an itinerant drunk, a stranger walking into our big breakup scene. He thwarted this plan.

"I'm Joe, his fucking guru. Or is it a gnu? The God-like or what-have-you. About to get sacked by the teeny tiny people but, hey ho, to hell with all that. I see all with this third eye of mine, the eye in the pyramid of my mind. And I see a Jezebel going about her business, delivering the sting. To thereafter walk the earth oblivious to the pain and the hurt, but the sting remaining for the rest of time and ever after. Do you know that pain? Have you been near the flame? Has he ever held you over that pit, deserted you a little bit maybe, made you suffer? Or perhaps it was someone else, before, could have been. Who knows? Not I. Your life is yours, mine is mine."

"How come you've got a black eye?" I asked, hoping this might bring him to his senses.

"Do you know your Greek? Polyphemus maybe or Phineus, the blinded king of Thrace, tortured every day by those horrible harpies for daring to defy Zeus when he revealed the future to all and sundry? It's the in thing, the vogue, to have but one eye. It be a signifier of wisdom, experience. They come on bended knee to touch the cloth."

"What happened?"

"I got into a, shall we say, 'discussion', with a man in that pub over there, The Roebuck, and he punched me in the face, quite hard. All very prosaic and boring, actually."

I told him we were about to leave. He appeared to be on the verge of falling asleep, slumped in his seat. I prodded him.

"Where are you staying tonight?"

He giggled. I wrote down the name of a nearby hotel on a beer mat and pressed it into his hand.

"Get along there, you'll find a bed for the night."

He stirred: "Honesty, always honesty. None of that flannel. Do you hear me?"

"I hear you."

"You do know what I'm talking about, don't you?"

"Writing."

"That's it," he said.

He managed to focus on Sarah.

"He's not bad, you know, at writing" he said. "Rough around the edges, for sure, and missing a bit of sinister cynicism but there's promise."

"I've heard," she said.

"Have you heard about anything else?"

"What do you mean?"

"Have you heard about love, for example?"

He fluttered his eyes, pursed his lips and seemed to be making a flapping bird with his hands. Sarah smiled the smile I'd captured at the National Trust place, when she was by the lake.

"What a lovely smile," said Joe.

I noticed a tear leaking down his cheek.

"She knows love, this girl, real love. Can't you see it? She's a believer. Perhaps we're mere pretenders, philosophisers. She is what we want to be but never shall. So, she's smashed your heart to pieces but has she not shown you the way, the love, and drowned you in it for more than long enough? This is how it should be."

"You weren't saying that in the pub before."

"Wasn't I? When was before anyway? What does it mean? So, I might have been bitter. It weighs heavy. It has to when you're cursed with this curse. It be a Logan stone across your heart, soil and muck burying you deep. It takes a lot of alcohol, a lot of freeing up, to see what is to be seen. Love is pure and honest. Has to be. Only the meek get pinched. The bold survive, as the redoubtable Ferris Bueller told us. The heart rules the head, has to. They don't mean any harm, these penny princesses. They're called from above and beyond to fulfil a destiny. They may pass themselves off as delicate little things, brush of a butterfly's wing and all that, but, as that very ugly and cousin-marrying Eleanor Roosevelt told us, women are like teabags and their true strength is not to be noticed until they find themselves in hot water. Of course, they fuck up but they do it with a good and honest if catastrophically malfunctioning heart. That's why they make the same mistakes again and again, dropping the good guy, passing him over, moving on to new fields aplenty. But, mere folly, I tell you. Hear my words, slurred as they may be: women, especially those with a mile wide smile, are beyond reproach."

He stopped talking and clumsily lit up a cigarette.

"I didn't know you smoked," I said.

"There are a lot of things you don't know about me. In fact, there are a lot of things you don't know about most people," he said.

"You won't be able to smoke in pubs for much longer if the government gets its way" I said, again in the hope of diverting him to more mundane thoughts.

He stared at Sarah.

"You loved this man, didn't you, with all your beating heart?"

"Yes."

"There. You were fucking loved, my dear frat-pal. In a world of concrete and steel, plagues and rats, you had your time, your turn. You were loved, man. By a good woman. She listened to you. You laid down together at night. You became one in this fight against the grabbers and the spoilers. How beautiful is that? I know it's hard to accept—what an understatement!—your first dumping. All that loving and giving, denuding. It feels like a forever promise. And it is, kind of, in the moment at least. And the moment after that. That's all we can be, ultimately. How can we tell the future, how feelings will wash up against us, change us? You plug in when you love, you merge, you really do become one. So when it ends, bang, you're suddenly plugged out, all these entrails of emotions trailing on the floor. The pain of your suffering is commensurate with the joy you took from the loving. Measure it, cherish it. I know you're messed up right now but love functions, it beats, and it will come back home. You will love again and be loved again, I promise. You have to be brave and walk across this earth looking and seeing and engaging. And from the messy morass someone else will rise and you'll be again, that extra alive, skyscraper happy, giddy on high. I know because I'm there now. I have that woman. I have that love. Believe me, man, it happens. And when, kiss of the Gods, it happens to you, you must not, for the sake of your sanity and the potential bricked up hours of guilt, overly concern yourself with the man you will inevitably usurp. He has lost her for a because that cannot be qualified or reasoned. He didn't do the small bits so they fell from the wall, fell from her heart. That was not your doing. Leave him behind, as we have each been left behind before. It is the way of a sensitive man, a writer, to imagine everything from all sides, especially the pain, to cry and think and fathom and heal for the world. He cannot do that, it corrodes the soul. He must stand alone, be heroic once or twice in his life, take what is gifted without looking for the coils and springs and mess in its trail, question it not. And, don't forget, some men are idiots. They deserve their pain. They deserve you to take their girl from them. They are careless and cruel. They talk down to them. They ignore them. They look at them as if they are dirt when they are among their friends. They say hurtful things. They try to punish them with their indifference or sulking. They manipulate. It will be your natural inclination to pity and excuse these men too, when you are sleeping with their wives. They don't have any right to sprinkle this bag of nails in your skull. Their tears are for themselves. They are babies, boy-men at best. They cry for themselves because they are alone and afraid more than because of the love they have lost. True love lets go, let's fly, accepts."

He closed his eyes and held such a beatific smile it seemed as if a film was being projected on to the underside of his eyelids. Perhaps Rachel was running towards him through a field of wild flowers, the sun shining fuzzy bright. Sinclair, college, woe upon woe, all gone. I looked at Sarah and motioned with my head that we should leave.

"Will he be all right?" she asked.

"I think so."

"We can't leave him"

I leaned over and spoke directly into his face.

"Will you be okay if we go now?"

He stirred.

"Of course, but before you leave, please hear me out. All this is really not about what it might appear to be about. As always, it's actually about living and dying. We all do it and always will. We are ever self-defining, measuring ourselves out, our lives. And we want, at the end, to feel it was worthwhile, feel that we counted for something. This is especially so with writers, the most foolish of all the fools. How many lovers have we had? How well have we loved or been loved? Tally it up. It is the only thing that makes a fraction of sense when, we know, there is no sense to be had. We live and we die. And in a hundred years no one will remember any of us. They will see our names on gravestones and that will be it; they will think nothing of the days we have spent, skies we have toiled and laughed under, friends we have shared. How stupid we are to consider ourselves precious and special. We have built cathedrals and mosques, beautiful and expansive, to form a rampart against the futility of life. All that splendour, all that time and effort and money. Dress it up high, in gold, intricately chiselled stone and meticulously carved wood. Sing fantastic hymns, script incredible liturgies and, hope on hope, it may resemble what is on the other side, ease you through. The folly of mankind! We know, all of us, even the preacher men in flowing robes, *especially* the preacher men in flowing robes, what is waiting for us. The worms and the beetles will have us and the bacteria from inside. We will rot down into the soil. No wonder they build palaces to save us from this truth!"

"Cheerful stuff," I said.

"Exactly! That's the paradox. Why can't we see it for what it is, stare it down? Knowing what awaits us should make us grasp at life's fading light, every single wonderful colourful noisy moment. We have around us all that cant, about living for the moment, you only get one chance and so on, but who hears that stuff? And if they do, it slips their mind in a minute or so, becomes a tiny fillip, a full stop in their book of the day. We have to really believe it, cherish it until we swoon on the beauty of being alive; every single bloody second. For it will soon be gone, soon vanished. It's the best we can do, the only thing that has a chance of saving us when our eyes close for the last time: well, I gave it my best shot, did what I wanted, made a difference, ate it all up, yum yum."

I asked again if he minded if we left.

"I can think and talk, can't I, and walk around? I'll find my way to this bloody blighted hotel you've recommended. And there I will sleep well, the drink kissing me sweet. I've always envied people who sleep easily. Their brains must be cleaner, the floorboards of the skull well swept, all the little monsters closed up in a trunk at the foot of the bed. I'm alone, of course, but Rachel is with me in spirit. You go. Please. Let me be. There will be no more hubbub."

"You sure?"

"Yes, please go. You are not my keepers."

As we moved away Sarah whispered:

"Does he always talk like that?"

"Like what?" (I wanted to see how she would describe him).

"A weird 19th century poet or someone out of a Shakespeare tragedy."

"He's usually a bit flowery but I've never heard him like that before. I've never heard anyone like that before."

"What, drunk? And mad?"

"I'd say he was more a visionary."

It had started to rain. I held out my hands to catch a few drops.

"I hope it all works out for you," she said. "And, promise me that you won't turn out like that man in there."

"But he's quite a famous writer, or was."

"Doesn't make him a nice person."

I didn't know whether to kiss her, hold her or shake her hand. She looked at me, expecting, I think, one of the three. It didn't seem fair that it was being left to me to decide when she'd engineered the whole scene; surely that was her responsibility.

"I'm going now," I said.

"Okay."

I'd drunk too much to drive so set off for the bus station. It was that peculiar hour when the daytime people, the workers and the shoppers, give way to the night-time people heading to bars and restaurants, dressed smartly, talking loudly and with purpose in their stride. The rain had brought with it a wind which was picking up wrappers and leaflets, causing them to revolve in small circles. The busker on the walkway played his guitar earnestly. I scanned the view across from the bus station. Pigeons were pecking hard at discarded fish and chips. Two down-and-outs were arguing, sitting on a wall. A young mum walked by pushing a pram, her hair in a scraped back ponytail. The rain was falling steadily now and acted like pencil lines scrubbing out a picture. I felt for the phone in my pocket. Was it shameless to ring Kate at such a time? I could make up a story of how, since I'd finished her, I'd realised I had made a big mistake and wanted to be with her, and so much so that I had been prepared to end my relationship with Sarah. The ruse would be relatively easy to carry out, though, naturally, I imagined she'd be sceptical for a while. I could deal with that. I began scrolling through the contacts in my phone. I got to 'K' and stalled, froze. I was snapped from reverie when a bloke walked past, trailed by a boy of about eight years old.

"Dad," the kid said. "How big will the bus be?"

His dad stretched out his arms.

"That's not very big."

"Watch this, then."

The man shuffled across the aisle in the bus station, his arms still outstretched as if multiplying the distance several times to show the length of a bus. I laughed. I reached for my phone again. I scrolled one letter back from 'K' to 'J' and stabbed out a text to Jenny:

'Please ask that Niall if he fancies a day out tomorrow.'

ALSO PUBLISHED BY POMONA

RULE OF NIGHT

Trevor Hoyle

ISBN 1-904590-01-2

If the Sixties were swinging, the seventies were the hangover — darker, nastier, uglier—especially if you lived on a council estate in the north of England. *Rule of Night* was first published in 1975 and has since become a cult classic. It pre-dates the vogue for 'hard men' and 'football hoolie' books by 25 years. It is, however, much more than this. Trevor Hoyle creates a chillingly detailed world, where teenagers prowl rainy fluorescent-lit streets dressed as their *Clockwork Orange* anti-heroes. The backdrop is provided by Ford Cortinas, Players No.6, the factory, and the relentless struggle to maintain hope. Hoyle, who has since been published by John Calder (home to Samuel Beckett and William S. Burroughs), has added a fascinating afterword to his original book which has been out of print and highly sought-after for many years.

FOOTNOTE*

Boff Whalley

ISBN 1-904590-00-4

Footnote* is clever, funny and irreverent—a story about a boy from the redbrick clichés of smalltown England reconciling Mormonism and punk rock, industrial courtesy and political insurrection.

He finds a guitar, anarchism and art terrorism and, after years (and years and years) of earnest, determined, honest-to-goodness slogging, his pop group† makes it big; that's BIG with a megaphone actually. They write a song that has the whole world singing and, funnily enough, it's an admirable summary of a life well lived—about getting knocked down and getting back up again.

Meanwhile, there's a whole world still happening: authentic lives carefully drawn, emotional but not sentimental and always with a writer's eye for detail. Footnote is not another plodding rock memoir but a compassionate, critical and sometimes cynical account of a life steeped in pop culture, lower division football and putting the world to rights.

* See page 293.

†Boff Whalley is a member of Chumbawamba.

THE FAN
Hunter Davies
ISBN 1-904590-02-0
The Fan is a collection of very personal, unusual pieces about his life as a supporter. He observes football in its sovereignty of the late 1900s and early 2000s and tackles the big topics of the day: Beckham's haircuts, high finance, the price of pies, the size of match day programmes, the enormous wages, the influence of Sky TV and England's numerous managers. Along the way, he also lets us into his home life, in London and the Lake District, his family, his work, his tortoise, his poorly knee (caused by too much Sunday football). Originally published in the *New Statesman*, *The Fan* catches Davies at his very best and most amusing. It will appeal to supporters of any age, sex and loyalties. The ultimate bedside football book.

Hunter Davies is one of Britain's most acclaimed writers and journalists. He has written over 30 books, among them modern classics, *The Beatles* and *A Walk Around The Lakes*. *The Glory Game*, published in 1972, is a benchmark work on football and is still in print today.

LOVE SONGS
Crass
ISBN 1-904590-03-9
"Our love of life is total,
everything we do is an expression of that,
everything that we write is a love song."
- Yes Sir, I Will
Crass: a rural-based anarchist collective formed in 1977 of a diverse and eclectic group of individuals who operated for several years using art, literature, film and music as vehicles to share information and ideas. They also wanted to change the world. This is a collection of words spanning those seven short years; a book of shock slogans and mindless token tantrums. An anthology of passionate love songs that sought to inspire a generation, and succeeded. This project has been carried out with the full co-operation of Crass members.

DIARY OF A HYPERDREAMER VOLUME 1
Bill Nelson

ISBN 1-904590-06-3

Bill Nelson is one of Britains' most respected creative forces. He came to prominence in the 1970s with Be Bop Deluxe and later, Red Noise. He has collaborated with like-minds such as Yellow Magic Orchestra, David Sylvian, Harold Budd and Roger Eno and still releases a prolific amount of new music.

Diary of a Hyperdreamer is his day-by-day journal in which he ponders on life, art and the nation. His unique perspective is fed by a career creating and producing music, photography, painting and video.

Written from his home in a hamlet in North Yorkshire, he also includes engaging details of his family life, regular musings on mortality, along with reflections on his childhood and former life as a globe-trotting 'pop star'.

KICKED INTO TOUCH
Fred Eyre

ISBN 1-904590-12-8

Fred Eyre's sporting life began full of promise when he became Manchester City's first ever apprentice. He never made their first team. In fact, he seldom made anyone's first team. Injuries played a part but limited talent was the greater curse. As he plummeted down the leagues he had something few footballers possess: a stud-sharp memory and an ability to write humorously about the sport he loves. Originally published in 1981, *Kicked Into Touch* has become an enigma—selling more than a million copies yet still retaining cult status within the sport and among fans. This new version has been completely revised, extended and updated with a new cover and set of photographs included.

It is set to reach a new generation of football fans looking for an antidote to the glib reportage of a sport lost to show business.

LOOKS AND SMILES
Barry Hines
ISBN 1-904590-09-8

Looks and Smiles was first published in the bad old days of the early 1980s when the nefarious Margaret Thatcher ruled Britain. High fashion was a L.E.D digital watch the size of a phone box and £23.50 a week on a Y.O.P Scheme was considered more than adequate, young man.

Mick Walsh, the book's central character, is a good kid who happens to be born at the wrong time in the wrong place. He wants to learn how to be a motorcycle mechanic, but bad luck, inexperience, and tough economic times prevent him from getting a job. At a disco one evening, he meets and dances with Karen Lodge whose future is similarly bleak. She works in the local shoe shop and the pair hang out with Mick's buddy, Alan, who joins the army and ends up policing Northern Ireland.

As ever, Hines avoids sentimentality and tells it like it is, without ever relinquishing hope and sympathy for his characters. *Looks and Smiles* is a classic piece of work, a gritty and poignant bulletin from a forgotten period of British history.

THE PRICE OF COAL
Barry Hines
ISBN 1-904590-08-X

Cast your mind back to the 1970s when Britain still had a coal industry and Margaret Thatcher had yet to do her worst. *The Price of Coal* brings the Yorkshire miners' existence vividly to life in a novel by turns tough, humorous and chilling. Centred around the daily grind at Milton colliery, a visit by the Prince of Wales provides the opportunity for well-aimed swipes at middle-management as they grass over the slag heaps, whitewash the blackened walls and put soft soap in the toilets. But when disaster strikes, Hines brings the reader face-to-face with the horror.

On its original publication, *The Price of Coal* was rightly lauded by *New Statesman* as 'a rare novel that stands out' and it has lost none of its stark power. Adapted for television as two linked plays, directed by Ken Loach as part of the much-missed Play For Today strand, the novel ranks alongside Hines' uncompromising classic, *A Kestrel for a Knave*.

MEAN WITH MONEY
Hunter Davies

ISBN 1-904590-13-6

At last, a book about money that tells it straight: put it under the bed. All of it. Sure, it makes for easy access to burglars but better them than the felons passing themselves off as financial advisors or acting as foot-soldiers for organisations with words like union, mutual, trust, alliance, equitable or assurance in their name.

Mean With Money, inspired by Hunter Davies' well-loved column in *The Sunday Times*, is wilfully short on practical advice but offers instead good humour and much-needed empathy as we face the corporate horror of high-handed and indifferent financial institutions

Davies, one of Britain's most celebrated writers, also looks at ingenious ways to save money (cut your own hair, for starters) and what to do with it when it arrives. Along the way, he reveals details of his regular visits to McDonald's (it's free to use their toilets), the eccentric old ladies who staff his local Oxfam shop and the swim that cost him £333. Famous for seminal works on The Beatles, football, and subjects as diverse as lottery winners and walking disused railway tracks, Davies is, once more, on top form.

ZONE OF THE INTERIOR
Clancy Sigal

ISBN 1-904590-10-1

'The book they dared not print', *Zone of the Interior* is a lost classic of zonked-out, high-as-a-kite Sixties literature. It tells the story of Sid Bell, an American political fugitive in London, who falls under the spell of Dr. Willie Last (modelled on the radical 'anti-psychiatrist' RD Laing).

This unlikely duo feast on LSD, mescaline, psilocybin and psychobabble, believing that only by self-injecting themselves with schizophrenia will they become true existentialist guerrillas. Their 'purple haze' odyssey takes them into the eye of the hurricane — mental hospitals, secure units for the violent, the Harley Street cabal of the 'Sacred 7' and semi-derelict churches that come complete with an underground tank for the woman convinced she's a fish.

THE ARMS OF THE INFINITE
Christopher Barker
ISBN 1-904590-04-7

The memoirs of Christopher Barker, the son of the cult writer Elizabeth Smart (*By Grand Central Station I Sat Down and Wept*) and the poet, George Barker.

He beautifully relates the inner-workings of a Bohemian up-bringing and offers an intriguing insight into one of the century's most important writers.

Although he is primarily a photographer, Christopher is himself a gifted writer and an early draft of his memoir formed a cover story for the literary magazine, *Granta*.

THE SECOND HALF
Hunter Davies
ISBN 1-904590-14-4

Sing it loud: there's only one Hunter Davies, one Hunter Davies. And he's still, in all fairness , Gary, bang on top form, doing well, the lad.

The Second Half is another collection of his personal pieces from the *New Statesman* covering three domestic seasons: the Euro Championship of 2004 and the 2006 World Cup when he unexpectedly became Wayne Rooney's top buddy.

"When a player gets sent off shouldn't we fans get some of our money back?" ponders Davies in one piece. "I just wish he'd shave his stupid face," he berates Jose Mourhino in another. And goooaaal!, Hunter rumbles Sven early doors: 'He's a spare swede at a veggie gathering. What is the point of him?' he writes two years before England's World Cup debacle.

As ever, his outlook is fiercely that of the fan — disgruntled, bewildered and passionate —wondering what the players do with all that money, all those girls, and why match programmes are 'full of adverts or arselicks for sponsors.'

BELIEVE IN THE SIGN

Mark Hodkinson

ISBN 1-904-59017-9

Believe in the Sign is about a damp corner of England where nothing much but everything happens. It is a 'sort of a memoir' of a normal, average boy who would have grown up happily average and normal but for a dark and perverse passion: the seductive lure of masochistic devotion to a no-hope, near-derelict football club.

But it isn't all joyously uplifting. Swimming through the murk is a swarm of snapshots that bring growing up in the 1970s and 1980s into startling focus. Mad kids and sad kids and good kids from broken homes; teenage wrecking parties; pub brawls; long existential marches along the motorway banking; the baiting of Elton John and a club chairman caught playing 'away from home.'

Then Death bumps into Life. A girl is abducted and the town becomes a cave, the light sucked out. Meanwhile in the sunny shine outside, the future is afoot: cotton mills close down and supermarkets invade; school-leavers evolve into YOP-fodder and everyone's mum is holding Tupperware parties to get the down-payment on a colour telly.

THE NOT DEAD

Simon Armitage

ISBN 978-1-904-59018-7

Simon Armitage issues a collection of work focusing on conflicts aside from the Great War and World War Two.

The poems were originally aired on a Channel 4 documentary of the same name, shown in the summer of 2007. They are featured alongside an introduction from Simon and press reviews of the film.

The work focus on the testimonies of veterans of the Gulf, Bosnia and Malayan wars, ex-soldiers who have seldom been heard before.

THE RICHARD MATTHEWMAN STORIES
Ian McMillan & Martyn Wiley
ISBN 978-1-904590-21-7

For a Yorkshireman who has spent half a lifetime in his native pit village, moving south is a mixed blessing and it is where Richard Matthewman's memories begin as he looks back with affection, humour, and no small measure of exasperation at forty-two summers— and bitter winters.

From boyhood through adolescence to marriage and a family, his stories are filled with a rich gallery of characters. Written by the broadcaster Ian McMillan and his friend, the late Martyn Wiley.

THIS ARTISTIC LIFE
Barry Hines
ISBN 978-1-904590-22-4

These short stories, many previously unpublished, cover sport and reflections on his home village of Hoyland Common in Barnsley, its landscape and the colourful characters that people it. Most of the pieces were written at the same time as his seminal novel, *Kes* which has been a staple of English literature for fifty years.

Also included is a series of poems, both whimsical and profound, and reflections on Hines' work by younger writers, Richard Benson and Mark Hodkinson.

THE LAST MAD SURGE OF YOUTH
Mark Hodkinson
ISBN 978-1904590200

Set in both the present day and the early 1980s, when new wave kids were dreaming up insurrection, *The Last Mad Surge of Youth* is about bands, growing up, moving away and getting famous, suicide, staying at home and getting bored, fanzines, the bomb, love, alcoholism, egotism and self-doubt.

The narrative begins with the D-I-Y ethos of punk, steering through major label hype, to tired aftermath.

JD SALINGER: A LIFE RAISED HIGH
Kenneth Slawenski

ISBN 978-1904590231

JD Salinger, A Life Raised High by American writer, Kenneth Slawenski, is the first major biography on Salinger by a UK based publisher.

Slawenski is a world-renowned expert on Salinger—he has run the *Dead Caulfields* website for more than fifteen years, widely thought of as the most authoritative Salinger site. He devoted seven years to researching and writing the book.

He conducted over sixty interviews and trawled libraries for letters, birth certificates, marriage licences and work records. The result is a definitive biography, looking both at Salinger's work in forensic detail, but also his family background and personal life.

DOWN THE FIGURE 7
Trevor Hoyle

ISBN 978-1904590255

Trevor Hoyle's fictional memoir reinforces the saying that the past is another country, with its own strange customs and mysterious rituals. None stranger and more mysterious than the secret world of childhood. Take a time trip back to the black-and-white 1950s, to a northern cotton town struggling to emerge from a decade of shortages and rationing, of make-do-and-mend.

But the war and its aftermath casts a long shadow. Gangs of feral youth, inflamed by the exploits of Hollywood tough guys, fed on *Movietone News* and the tales of dads and uncles who served in the Forces, are still fighting the Nazzies and the Nips – and each other – on the bits of wasteland between the streets and houses. It all seems very innocent (even the fumbling exploration of sex behind the garages) and indeed it is. Until Terry Webb's uncle turns up, ex-Desert Rats, and brings a piece of the war home with him.

MY IMPROPER MOTHER AND ME
Esther Fairfax
ISBN: 978-1-904590-26-2
Lotte Berk was one of the most extraordinary women of our times. She became world famous as the devisor of the Lotte Berk Technique, a revolutionary fitness programme that led her to great fame and wealth during the 1960s and 1970s.

Among her students were a swathe of movers and shakers — Britt Ekland, Maureen Lipman, Geraldine McEwan, Zoe Wanamaker, Shirley Conran, Edna O'Brien, Prue Leith and Sian Phillips.

This is a compelling portrait of the outrageous German émigré by her daughter, Esther Fairfax. It reveals the inner workings of a Bohemian life lived to the extreme. Cajoled to dance naked in Paris at the age of sixteen. Fairfax's remarkable story embraces drug addiction, sexual liberation, poverty, isolation, fame, and finally, hope.

WEIRDO. MOSHER. FREAK.
The Murder of Sophie Lancaster
Catherine Smyth
ISBN: 978-1-904590-27-9
Twenty-year-old Sophie Lancaster was kicked to death by a pack of 'feral' youths at her local park in Bacup, Lancashire. Her boyfriend, Rob Maltby, was also set upon and received serious injuries.

Their only 'crime' was to dress differently, as 'goths' or 'moshers' in the easy shorthand of the media, which cited the killing as another example of Broken Britain.

Catherine Smyth was the first reporter on the scene and remained at the heart of the story throughout. A mother herself, she writes evocatively of the impact it had on both the Lancaster family and Bacup itself.

Profits from sales of this book will be divided equally between the author, publisher and The Sophie Lancaster Foundation.

THE CELESTIAL CAFÉ
Stuart Murdoch
ISBN: 978-1904590248

The debut book by Stuart Murdoch, the founder member and singer of the popular indie band, Belle and Sebastian. Stuart writes evocatively of life on the road in an international touring band, contrasting it with his homespun and reflective returns back home to Glasgow.

BLACK ROSES: THE KILLING OF SOPHIE LANCASTER
Simon Armitage
ISBN 978-1-904590-29-3

Black Roses is a poetic sequence written in the voice of Sophie Lancaster. The radio broadcast of *Black Roses* won the BBC Radio Best Speech Programme of 2011 and was shortlisted for the Ted Hughes Award for Poetry. One-third of all profits from the sale of this book will be donated to the Sophie Lancaster Foundation.

DIARY OF A HYPERDREAMER, VOL 2
Bill Nelson
ISBN: 978-1904590316

Now in his sixties and living with his Japanese wife, Emi, in rural Yorkshire, Nelson spends his days making music, dreaming, scheming and fretting. In these verbatim entries from his diary he also reflects, with great tenderness, on the early death of his younger brother, Ian, a fellow musician. Elsewhere, he ponders... on human nature:

Why is it that gentleness and sensitivity are in short supply whilst cynical spite and small-mindedness flourishes?

on the joy of life:

I had a ball simply looking and feeling. Wow! And I remembered our youth and those times and that music and I was grateful to be alive and to have lived through those times. Ain't life grand when you're in the mood for it to be so?

BOY INTERRUPTED
Dale Hibbert
ISBN-13: 978-1904590309

"I have felt alone all my life." Dale Hibbert's story reads like a song by The Smiths, which might not be a coincidence.

His mother died when he was eight days old. He was a latch-key kid. He has married four times and has eight children. He has 'died' twice. He is a depressive. He has been penniless. But he has also been a musician, producer, sound engineer, a millionaire and the owner of night clubs, cafés and successful businesses. He has lived in a car, and a mansion.

Hibbert was a member of The Smiths during their early days and privy to the dreams and outlandish ideas of young Morrissey and Marr. As the bass player and engineer at their first recording sessions, he helped shape their sound. With Morrissey's arms around his waist, they rode the streets of Manchester.

Hibbert gives a compelling insight into the rain-swept, working class life that fuelled the creativity of The Smiths.